THEY PLOTTED REVENGE AGAINST AMERICA

ABE F. MARCH

ALL THINGS
THAT MATTER
PRESS

THEY PLOTTED REVENGE AGAINST AMERICA

Copyright © 2009 by ABE F. MARCH

This is a work of fiction; any resemblance to actual persons, living or dead, is unintentional.

ISBN: 0-9822722-2-7

ISBN13: 978-0-9822722-2-0

LIBRARY OF CONGRESS CONTROL NUMBER: 2009921282

Cover design by All Things That Matter Press

Published in 2009 by All Things That Matter Press

Printed in the United States of America

This story stuck with me. In fact, after reading it, I thought about it every time I approached a chicken dinner.
Of course, it's just a story, but it could happen.

Two Iraqi youths (one Christian and one Muslim) lose their homes and their entire families during the invasion of Iraq and vow revenge.

They, along with a group of other young Palestinian men and women with similar pasts, are recruited for a terrorist plot to infect American poultry, water fowl and fish with a deadly virus that mutates to humans.

The author is a recognized expert on the Middle-East, and through his characters he presents interesting insights into the Israeli-Palestinian conflict and the global politics that keeps this international powder keg so near the flames of discontent.

"They Plotted Revenge" is a suspenseful blend of intrigue and romance, complete with a double agent working with the Israeli Secret Service. He masterminds the plot, but as the day of infestation nears, Homeland Security begins to close in on him. At the same time some of the people recruited to plant the virus become acquainted with a few Americans and realize their actions could kill millions of innocent citizens ignorant of actual events in the Middle-East. Most of them back out and head for home.

One, however, decides to carry out the plot, even after it is officially cancelled. To find out what happens next, you'll have to read to book.
This is a story for our times, and it makes some pertinent points about the Middle-East conflict that threatens us all.

- **Ron Kruger,** newspaper columnist for over 30 years and author of A Higher Good

They Plotted Revenge is an intriguing read, and one that left the hair on the back of my neck standing up. It's one thing to think of a war "over there" that is more out of sight and out of mind than we care to admit. It's another thing altogether to realize that the actions that have led us to this point in history could actually be unstoppable.

This story – part fiction and a whole lot of real – is about an attack set to take place in the US, right under our noses. It isn't about bombs going off, or folks firing guns and rockets at one another. This is about getting at the very foundation of our own survival.

Iraqi youths from different backgrounds within their own country are recruited as covert operators of a frightening army. They are trained to blend in, become part of the society that they are preparing to unravel. They are tasked with infecting America's food and water with a deadly virus that can mutate to humans, and for which there may not be a ready cure in time, or at a price that we can afford. Working for someone who turns out to be a double agent, at first glance they seem just like young couples anywhere, and all of them are prepared to give up their lives for their cause. As they get to know the Americans that they hide among however, some of them lose heart and decide not to go through with the plan, but in the world that we live in, there will always be someone that will see a project through to the end, even after the battle has ended.

Author Abe F. March provides us with a safe haven – a good book – to read, discuss and explore what's really happening, and this is a book you'll want to make time for.

- **Pam Robertson**, Ph.D. Author of *Marching Across the Heart*, and the newly published short story *Catch You Later*.

Dedication

This book is dedicated to all those struggling for a better life free of conflict.

Special thanks go to:

Gene Fegely, my H.S. classmate for his early review and suggestions.

Mary Appia, for her candid critique that influenced numerous changes.

Ramzi Edward Nari, for his insights about life in Iraq.

Sylvia Greunewalt for her technical assistance

My two daughters, Caroline and Christine, for their support in my efforts.

My son Duane, for his historical input and editing assistance.

And to my wife, Gisela, whose patience and indulgence allowed me to finish the book.

CHAPTER 1

Fire and explosions illuminated the nighttime sky over Baghdad as bombs fell in quick succession. On the third floor of a six-story apartment building, Yussef huddled with his family in one corner of the living room, silent and trembling, shocked by what was happening.

It was common knowledge that pressure was placed on Saddam Hussein to comply with UN demands, but they believed their leader when he said that he didn't have what the West called Weapons of Mass Destruction (WMDs). They felt that the demand for inspections was an affront, and to be attacked was unthinkable. Now they were under siege and all they could do was stay indoors, pray, and wait for it to end. The screams of jet aircraft and the sounds of explosions were horrific.

Communications lines had been cut, presumably for security reasons, and the main power station had taken a direct hit. There was no way of knowing what was happening around them. Yussef's father tried to give comfort. The candlelight illuminated his face as he spoke softly, expressing his belief that only military targets would be hit. Yussef listened to his words but it did not diminish the fright in the eyes of his younger brother and sister as they sat holding on to each other without uttering a sound. The words of comfort vanished when another explosion shook the building. His mother smothered her screams with the pillow she was holding. It was too much. Yussef felt compelled to do something. He wanted to see what was happening outside and decided to make his way to his friend's house where he would have a good view of the surrounding area.

Yussef stood and said, "Father, I will find out what is happening. I will be back soon."

His father looked at him. He realized he was no longer a child but fully grown, educated - a son to make any father proud. The need to protect and comfort the rest of the family was his responsibility. He embraced him and said, "Be careful and don't stay away too long."

Yussef hurried down the stairwell and exited the building, stepping over debris on the sidewalk. People stared at him through shattered windows as he made his way along the empty street. He stayed close to the buildings and was half way to the next corner when the impact of an explosion knocked him down. He struggled to his feet looking in the direction of the blast and saw that the building where he lived had been hit. In panic, he ran back to his house. Darkness together with the unsettled dust made visibility difficult as he stepped over rubble blocking the main entrance. He fought to gain access by working his way around and over mangled objects until he reached the stairwell. He worked frantically in the dark interior to clear a path as he made his way up. Shouts and screams emanated from the first and second floors as he passed by. When he reached the third floor he stopped and gaped at the open space facing him. The rocket had made a direct hit on the third floor. The wall to the outside was no more. All he could see was rubble as he looked for signs of his family. He worked his way to where they had been sitting when he left them and at once knew their fate. The entire outside wall had been blown in on them. In frenzy he dug through the debris, pushing aside heavy cement blocks and support beams to locate them.

He was shattered by what he saw. One by one, he extricated the bodies and placed them side-by-side. He bent over each one, weeping, looking for any sign of life, oblivious to the continued bombardment. When his tears subsided, his thoughts turned to hate and revenge against those he held responsible.

***

Three blocks away in a high-rise apartment building, Ahmed had been playing backgammon with his cousin when the attack began. The noise and sudden illumination of the nighttime sky caused them to jump from their seats and run to the window.

The vantage point from the seventh floor gave them a wide view of the city. They stood together wide-eyed, witnessing the explosions and tracer bullets that hit supposed targets. At first it appeared to be strategic targeting of governmental buildings, but then bombs would land indiscriminately outside that area. Rockets were being launched from a distance as well as from fast moving aircraft. The view together with the deafening sounds of aircraft and explosions was something they could not have imagined. Saddam's anti-aircraft guns were blasting away incessantly, lighting up the sky with their tracers and adding to the sounds and confusion of the onlooker. They were mesmerized by it all. They too had heard the rumors, but no one really believed there would be an attack because most Iraqi civilians did not consider America an aggressor nation. Arab news propaganda had labeled America as an imperialist aggressor for decades. The Gulf War, although a UN action, was clearly led by the US, but the Americans had stopped its action when the objective was achieved. They had reminded themselves that America rarely initiated attacks or invaded other countries, but only acted in self-defense or in the defense of other nations. Yet now it was happening and they were shocked. Rescue vehicles with their sirens blaring could be heard amidst the din of the unabated onslaught.

"My God," said Ahmed, "They're destroying our city."

His cousin stood staring with his mouth hanging open. They were witnessing a live demonstration of America's air power that was awesome and devastating. Ahmed could see his home from where he stood. He could see other people in the surrounding buildings staring at the spectacle from their windows defying the logic of safety. Shattered glass mingled with the noise as the assault continued.

"I think I should go home," said Ahmed. His cousin nodded his head without saying a word or even turning. Just as Ahmed was about to turn away from the window, he saw the flash and heard the explosion. It happened so quickly. The fast moving jet launched the rocket as it went screaming by, making a direct hit on his home. In a panic he ran to the stairwell. Elevators were not working and the stairwell was crowded with residents carrying candles. He yelled for them to clear a path as he made his way down the seven floors to the street. Oblivious to his own safety, he ran through the open street to his home. Smoke was pouring out of the windows and the entrance to the building. People who lived on the lower level were coming out into the street coughing and clutching possessions. Those on the upper level where Ahmed's family lived were all trapped. It was then that he noticed the large gaping hole on the third floor where his friend Yussef lived.

***

In a back street café off Beirut's Hamra district, Ahmed and Yussef stared at each other across a small wooden table. Swatting at flies was an unconscious reaction to their perpetual nuisance. There were no screens in the open windows of homes or businesses and AC was a luxury for the rich and modern hotels.

The small movement of air from the slow rotation of the ceiling fan felt good. Few people were in the café at this hour and that suited their purpose. Ahmed diverted his gaze to the scarred walls, evidence of the armed conflicts in and around Beirut. His thoughts were on the decision he was about to make, a decision that would change his life and that of Yussef. They could still back out, but there was little chance of that: their desire for retaliation was too strong. Nothing stood in their way, since they had no family to worry about, yet it was a decision that would change their lives forever. They would be leaving the world they grew up in to start a new life in the West. Now that their initial training was completed, they had only to say yes in order to move on.

They had both decided to leave Iraq when their families were wiped out during America's assault on Baghdad. The memories of the tragedy could not be erased. Occupation of their country by foreign troops, primarily American, in and around Baghdad, only deepened their desire for vengeance. As they faced each other across the table, it was easy to read the thoughts of the other. They had grown up together, attended the University of Baghdad, and were in their final year to receive a degree in engineering. The future had looked bright for both of them. Although Ahmed was Christian and Yussef Muslim, religion played no role in their decision nor did it affect their friendship. They now shared the same anger and sorrow and were prepared to take their need for retribution into the heart of America. They believed their cause was just and the decision to go was now in their hands.

Speaking softly, Ahmed said, "I feel it is my duty to avenge my family. If America can invade our country, why should we not invade America?"

Yussef nodded his head and said, "I agree. Allah is a God of justice, and justice will be served."

Ahmed watched Yussef as he rubbed his chin. Yussef turned his head and was looking at the battle scars on the walls. Daylight shone through the visible shell holes while others were covered with picture frames. Yussef's goatee that he proudly wore would need to be shaved off before departing. In their new life they would need to act, walk, talk, and appear western to blend into the society. Yussef suddenly turned and looked directly into Ahmed's eyes. Ahmed's steady gaze didn't waver when he smiled and nodded his head. Ahmed reached across the table and took Yussef's hand in his. They continued to look into each other's eyes as they both nodded in the affirmative. They stood, embraced, and then asked the waiter for the check.

***

Their initial training had taken place in the outskirts of Beirut adjacent to a Palestinian refugee camp. There were a total of six men being trained for the mission. They all had the same thing in common: families lost to American or American-supported Israeli action. The Palestinians knew how futile it was to retaliate against Israel. It didn't accomplish anything other than create more martyrs. They wished to attack the country that supported, and often appeared to sponsor and condone, Israeli actions. During training they were reminded of the most recent Israeli attack on Lebanon in the summer of 2006 as yet another example of Israeli crimes that America refused to prevent. That action caused scores of deaths to Lebanese civilians. The Israeli invasion of Lebanon in the summer of 1982 left a multitude of scars. The physical scars were still evident, but the unseen psychological scars had taken deep root. Many of those who had been tolerant of western views changed their attitudes in the summer of 2006. The bombardment of downtown Beirut and the killing of many innocent civilians could not be forgotten. Young people whose families had fallen victim to these acts were ripe for recruitment and there was no shortage of candidates. They were united in believing that to condone aggression was the same as committing the act itself. Action against America was justified in retaliation for Israeli actions against Lebanon and the Palestinians.

In addition to Ahmed and Yussef, there were four other Palestinian trainees. Two would be designated as backup in the event something happened to any of the original four. The profiles of those chosen for the mission were those best suited to go to America. They all had a good education, which included at least one foreign language, and English was a requirement. Ahmed and Yussef both spoke fluent English and had also studied German at the university in Baghdad. It was for this reason that the second phase of their training would take place in Germany where they would begin their phase-in to western culture and could count on the support of the Muslim community there. They would become familiar with elements of the operation in a setting that would aid them in carrying out their mission. The exact nature of the mission had not yet been revealed, but they applied themselves diligently; their training had been vigorous and they took it seriously. The instructor was very specific: "You are not on a suicide mission. You are on Jihad, a crusade against America, and you will carry out justice." There had been no mention of the name Bin Laden or Al Qaeda in any of their training although they were all aware of the successful attack on the World Trade buildings. As far as they knew, their mission was an independent action. They didn't know who was sponsoring the mission nor did they care. They were focused on the need for revenge. Justification for the pending actions was continually reinforced in their training with facts about

America's history of supported aggression by Israel. In their first session, their instructor used a chart showing UN Resolutions against Israel.

"Here are listed 65 Resolutions against Israel, from 1955 to 1992, for its illegal activity and flagrant violations of international law. Further, since 1970, the US has vetoed 32 other resolutions that condemned Israel's acts or called on Israel to withdraw from the land it occupies. Of the UN Resolutions on the books against Israel, not one of them has ever been enforced. Why is it that UN Resolutions are applied against other countries like Iraq for allegedly having WMDs, while none of the UN Resolutions against Israel have been enforced? Is that just?"

The class responded with fists pounding on the tables yelling, "No. Death to the Americans and Israelis!"

"And what about the arsenal of WMDs that Israel possesses? Why is Israel not required to give up its weapons? I think you know the answer to that. You who are part of this mission will make sure that America can no longer escape by turning a blind eye to Israeli actions. They must be punished!"

CHAPTER 2
FIRST FLIGHT WEST

Ahmed and Yussef's flight to Frankfurt, Germany, took less than four hours. They were well dressed, clean-shaven and each carried a small suitcase. Their passports were Lebanese and the purpose of their visit, as stated on the visas, was as student tourists. They would be staying at a *Jugendherberge* - a youth hostel on the edge of the *Pfälzerwald* – the Palatine forest in southwest Germany. It was there that they would be contacted with further instructions.

They spoke little during the flight and were alert to everything around them. Despite their attitudes, it was exciting to be traveling west for the first time in their lives. They were full of anticipation for what lay ahead. Landing in Frankfurt, the busiest airport they had ever seen, was exciting. Aircraft with names from all over the globe could be seen parked at the terminal's loading ramps. When they disembarked they were immediately faced with the sound of the German language and could begin using the language they had studied. They followed the line of passengers that led them to customs control. The customs inspector stamped their passports and visas and handed them back with a pleasant grin. They retrieved their luggage but were stopped before exiting for inspection. The official asked them if they were carrying any items requiring payment of duty. They both said no. He asked them to open their luggage. He made a cursory inspection, all the while glancing at their faces. Satisfied, he told them that they could close their bags and proceed to the exit.

They were relieved. They were not carrying anything that was disallowed and had not been overly concerned since questions or inspections of any nature was something that they had been trained for and they took it in stride without any outward display of nervousness.

The instructions they carried together with directions to the youth hostel were easy to follow. The train ride was just another event that added to their new experience and the use of the language. They boarded the train at the airport that took them to the city of Mannheim. From there they took another train to Neustadt and then to Landau, their last stop in southwest Germany. A final bus ride and they arrived at the youth hostel, situated at the edge of the Pfälzerwald mountain range, with convenient access to forest hiking trails.

They were in the youth hostel just two days when contact was made. It was a surprise to both of them when a girl, dressed in athletic wear, approached them as they sat on the terrace having a cup of tea. Without any introduction she asked if they would like to join her for a jog. Their initial reaction was to decline, until she asked them in a lowered voice whether they had a pleasant flight from Beirut. Since no one else knew of their origin, they consented.

"You may wish to change into something more suitable for jogging," she said.

They excused themselves and went inside the hostel to change into the athletic wear they brought with them. Their curiosity was peaked wondering what would happen next.

The girl was waiting, and when she saw them emerge from the building, she motioned for them to follow as she turned and started down a path leading into the forest. As soon as they entered the forest, they commenced jogging. Ahmed and Yussef were both in top physical condition as was the girl. She had short brown hair and a well-developed athletic physique. Her features were pleasing to the eye yet there was nothing unusual about her face that would cause anyone to give her special notice. Her special qualities were not visible. Although there was a situation that had brought her to the attention of her boss, it was her intelligence and unique qualities that had placed her in the leadership role she now held.

At a fork in the trail she stopped jogging and pointed to a large rock formation. "These are called *Felsen*," she said. "These wooded hills are part of the *Pfälzerwald*. You will see many *Felsen* like this throughout the forest. There are numerous medieval castles in the *Pfälzerwald* and most were built on *Felsen* like these. For the most part, the castles are now just ruins – that's *Ruine*."

Ahmed and Yussef were fascinated with the country, so different from Iraq, and with all the new things facing them. They followed the girl as she began the climb to the large rock formation. As they drew near, they noticed a recess below one of the large boulders with a cave-like appearance. She led them into the recess where provisions were stored and offered them a place to sit. She said, "My name is Samantha. I am your contact and instructor for the next phase of your training. I will answer any relevant questions you may have. May I welcome to your new home in Germany." She extended her hand smiling graciously. They shook hands with the same politeness and identified themselves.

"You will be given a new identity shortly. You may be required to make some alteration in your appearance before we have pictures taken for your ID. Your new life has begun. I suggest you do not look back." She paused and then said, "Are there any questions?"

Ahmed shook his head and Yussef said, "I suppose you will tell us what our next step will be."

"I have your training program committed to memory. We will avoid whenever possible the use of written communication. Concentrate on your assignments so that the important things will be remembered. I will tell you what things must be memorized in detail. For now, we will take one day at a time. Your daily assignments will progressively increase with new activity. For the present, you will continue to stay at the hostel until I have arranged for your new identity cards."

She reached into her pocket and pulled out two maps of the *Pfälzerwald*, handing one to each of them. "The map shows the towns and villages in the surrounding area. Notice the network of hiking trails that are clearly marked throughout and take note of the numerous *Felsen* and the various *Ruine*. Some of them will be contact locations. I will advise you of other routes to follow that are not shown on these maps. Do not mark your maps with these alternate routes, but remember them by a simple code that I have devised. Your movements on the trails must appear normal to any hiker. The alternate routes will lead to predetermined *Felsen* where meetings will take place. Any questions?"

"No," said Ahmed. "Your instructions are very clear."

"And you, Yussef?" said Samantha.

"No questions."

"I will leave you now. Everything here is at your disposal. Study the maps and become familiar with the articles placed here. You will make your own way back to the hostel tonight. If you don't hear from me, return here tomorrow. I will be in contact with you."

She turned and left.

***

In another part of Beirut, training had just been completed with six women. Each of these women had families killed by western-supported aggression. They had no attachments that would cause them concern and were completely free to make their own decisions. They would be paired with the men who had simultaneously completed their initial training. The pairing process was still being analyzed and no determination had yet been made concerning their intended partners. The analysis dealt with personalities suitable for working together and the capabilities needed for the assignment. All factors were carefully being evaluated, and although the women would be in a support role, they would have the capability to take the lead role if or when required.

Culture had played a major role in the lives of these women and traditions were hard to ignore. Religion was also a factor that influenced the role of women in their society. Although this role in the past had been one of submission to men, education had changed their outlook. These were women determined to make it on their own, and the opportunity to do so was now available to them. They could satisfy their need for revenge and at the same time utilize their education for personal growth. They were ready for whatever was asked or demanded of them.

The initial training of both the men and the women included physical fitness in a combat-ready environment. The training was demanding, requiring proficiency in the use of firearms and martial arts. There was classroom instruction that dealt with the history of their people and their suffering. This was an important and an integral part of their instruction to reinforce and validate their mission. They were presented with selected portions of American history and its course of action in recent years. The women were given special training to prepare them with more assertiveness that would enable them to fill the role of a liberated woman in western society. Political history focused on the State of Israel and its imposition in the Arab world. It dealt with the unqualified moral and financial support given by the United States to the State of Israel that had given them the boldness to do most anything they wished without consequences. Those responsible for the Sabra and Chatila massacres in Lebanon still went unpunished. "And those of you in this class that lost their families in those massacres will have your chance to avenge those deaths," said their instructor. "You will help to punish those who committed these crimes and be serving justice."

***

David Levy sat in his field office studying the file of each trainee. It served to remind him that the project he was engaged in was real. After almost ten years of rising through the ranks within the Mossad organization he was about to change his life. The men he had selected for the mission were the brightest of all the candidates that had volunteered, and the strongest motivation driving them was their unwavering determination to punish. They would not be satisfied until they could inflict much damage on the aggressors who had invaded their lands and caused the death of their loved ones. His own reasons for directing this mission was something he had not revealed to anyone, but his need for retribution was as strong as any of the trainees. He had been selected to lead this group by a person previously unknown to him. He now had access to unlimited resources to carry out the mission and he could use it in whatever manner he chose.

David carried American and Israeli passports. It was one of the advantages of being Jewish. The right for dual citizenship was not available to most other Americans and that advantage would be useful for this undertaking. Total secrecy was employed in identifying and interviewing the candidates for the training. They were given limited information regarding the purpose of their initial interview, however once they were selected, they were provided with more information after pledging an oath of secrecy.

It was time to select two women as partners for his men in Germany. Natasha, the trainer for the group of women, was asked for the files of the two female candidates that she felt would best match the profiles of the two men.

After careful examination of the men's files, Natasha made her selection of two women that she felt would make a good match. Not only were they well educated, they also had the passion required to fulfill the assignment. In addition, she selected them for their pleasing appearance that would help to insure an acceptable, and hopefully agreeable, pairing with their intended partners. The profile of each trainee was also reviewed from a psychological perspective that included intelligence as well as compatibility with their assigned accomplices to support the male-led role. They were well suited for this position since it was inherent in their male dominated upbringing.

As with the men, the women were fully indoctrinated in the history of the Middle East region and the plight of the Palestinians caused by Israel's occupation of their land. They did not need to be reminded about the oppression of the Palestinians that continued unabated. Photos of dead loved ones were a constant reminder of their need for revenge. They knew about the acts of vengeance taken against Israel, but it had accomplished nothing. Even sacrificing lives in a suicide mission was futile. Israel always responded, and did so with a power ten-fold that only served to deepen the hatred and perpetuate the violence.

Natasha made a final review of her selected trainees and prepared to submit the files of Karla and Elham to David for his acceptance or rejection. If accepted, the girls would be sent to meet their designated partners at their new training location. The risk of a bad match was considered; however there would only be a recall in an extreme case. The girls knew what was expected of them and they would do their part to the best of their ability.

Natasha understood what it was like to start a new life. As she sat with the files in front of her she reflected on her own life and how she came to be where she was. Being born in a small Russian village had not diminished her desire for learning. She had excelled in her studies, which enabled her to go to Moscow for advanced education and further training. Her physical capabilities were another attribute that caused her to be selected to join a special branch of the armed services and eventually become part of an elite corps of women sharpshooters. Although she had excelled in her duties and desired to serve the land of her birth, she was suddenly categorized as politically unsuitable when it became known that she was a Jew. Trying to hide her Jewish heritage had worked for a time, but it had been no longer possible once she had gained notice from her superiors and was selected for foreign espionage training. This required a thorough background check and that had revealed her true heritage. It was the beginning of the end for Natasha and her family. She longed to live in freedom and be accepted as the person she was, and not judged by her religious heritage. When the opportunity presented itself, she immigrated with her family to Israel where she was told that she would be welcomed and free to live the life she chose. She was excited at this opportunity and soon volunteered to help other refugees get settled in Israel. She began working with Ethiopian immigrants and suddenly there were obstacles in getting them assimilated into Israel society. She found prejudice against these new settlers, yet the more she fought in their defense, the more she earned contempt from her Israeli colleagues. She soon became disillusioned with her work and the attitude of those in authority.

Her family had not been accepted with the open arms that they were promised, but made to feel inferior.

Over time Natasha witnessed the abuse and treatment of the Palestinians, and her own experience with discrimination caused her to have sympathy for them. Now instead of being persecuted herself, she was part of a society that was inflicting persecution on others. When she spoke out against this injustice, she was verbally abused and made to feel as an outcast. It was a "love it or leave it" edict. When she refused to conform, she lost her job and was relegated to menial work that provided little income, thus causing her family to live in a manner that was substandard even to their former Russian living conditions. The empathy she felt for her Jewish brethren who had suffered under the hands of the Nazis diminished as she saw them inflicting their own brand of oppression on the Palestinians. It was during this period of time that her sympathy towards the Palestinians grew. Nighttime phone calls with threats on her life did not daunt her; they were a spark that ignited her determination to devote her life in fighting for justice. She came to regard the Zionism practiced in Israel in many ways comparable with the attitudes of the Nazis. The practice of subjugation was intolerable to Natasha. She came to realize that the hopelessness of the Palestinian people stemmed from the oppression, murder, torture, mass deportation and stripping them of their humanity.

Yes, she thought. Justice will be served, and it will begin with these two people I have selected. She closed the files and transmitted the information to David through a secret coding device that he had supplied to her.

***

17

David was pleased as he reviewed the credentials of the two women Natasha had selected. He would have been more pleased if Natasha had indicated a preference for pairing Karla and Elham with Ahmed and Yussef, but he knew that was his responsibility. He was trained to evaluate people by a number of traits and characteristics that constituted a profile. Knowing he was about to make decisions that would change the lives of these trainees, he couldn't help but reflect on his own recruitment and how he came to be where he was.

Born in America, his life there and the events leading to this stage in his life seemed a long time ago. He remembered his first trip to Israel during a vacation from his studies. His fair skin and sandy-colored hair made him stand apart from most of those he had traveled with, but he felt as though he belonged. They were a small group of students to work at a kibbutz, an Israeli collective community that combines Socialism and Zionism in a form of Labor Zionism. He was excited to be working with others within this commune to help with Israel's growth. The horrors of the Holocaust would always be a reminder of suffering caused by bigotry, and to him it had special significance since his grandfather had been a victim. The group of students was further indoctrinated in the belief of Biblical rights to the entire land of Palestine. They were determined to help reclaim this territory, but the Palestinians remained an obstacle.

As he learned in the indoctrination, one course of action was to bring as many Jews as possible to Israel to settle, thus requiring more space and justifying expansion. That program had already brought Jews from many countries, and they were now feeling the need for more space. The second course of action, which was endorsed by the more radical youths, was piece-meal annexation by building settlements in Palestinian territory. Israel had acquired much additional territory in the 1967 war and did not intend to give it back. So far they had not been forced to comply with UN Resolutions calling for the return of the occupied territories.

They knew that world sympathy for the victims of the Holocaust was a good weapon to use when needed to deflect and divert attention away from their refusal to comply. More young people were sought to join their ranks to help them in their quest to blanket Palestine with Jewish settlements. The daily war against the Palestinians was one of intimidation and agitation intended to incite revolt. And when there was an attack, even when stones were thrown, the Israeli army would respond with heavy weapons. Incitement to violence was part of the training he received. Whenever world opinion would favor the Palestinians, an army of young people and volunteers was ready to antagonize the Palestinians into committing more acts that would help to justify Israel's need for expanded borders for security reasons.

David had returned to the states to complete his studies. After graduation from college, he moved to Israel and became an Israeli citizen. After completing compulsory military service, he joined the Mossad secret service. It was there that David became more knowledgeable about the politics of the region and their long range plans. It was also the duty of the Mossad to root out, and if necessary punish or even eliminate, those who would interfere with their plans. Mossad's motto was: "By way of deception thou shalt do war." That concept was practiced on many fronts. When he became disillusioned with his work, it was not a simple matter to resign from his post. His knowledge of the secrets within the organization could make him a potential adversary. He realized that it would be more advantageous to work from within the organization than from the outside. He could utilize the resources of the secret service to his advantage now that he was involved in a mission of his own. The true reason that caused him to seek revenge was a secret he kept to himself.

David made his decisions and placed the folders aside. He was pleased to be part of this action that would help him overcome a feeling of intense guilt. Keeping the west engaged in their long range plans by devious means was more involved than he wished to acknowledge.

***

David chose the name James Frey as the new identity for Yussef. Mr. Frey's background would reflect that he was born in Mainz, Germany, that he was an only child, and that his parents were both deceased.

Ahmed's new identity would be Albert Roth, showing that he was born in Augsburg, Germany, and that he was an only child. His background would reflect that his father was killed in an automobile accident and that his mother was living in a care facility having been diagnosed with Alzheimer's disease.

For the women, he gave Elham an identity as Mary Schneider, and to Karla he gave her the name, Brenda Fischer. Their background information was carefully researched and placed on file.

David arranged for passport size photos of the trainees. He instructed them in the style and color of their hair as well as the clothes they should wear for the photos. His ability to create authenticity in passports was part of David's capability within his organization. He would first have German identification cards created for the four individuals. They would need them to move about freely and get accustomed to the use of their new names.

David traveled to Frankfurt to meet with Samantha. Meeting with her always brought back some unpleasant memories, yet there was also an attraction that he kept to himself. At that meeting he presented her with the ID's of the four trainees and gave her instructions regarding the next phase of their training. He further informed her that "Mary Schneider" and "Brenda Fischer" would be arriving the following day and that she was to meet them at the airport. They would be traveling on Lebanese passports with student visas. Samantha was to make arrangements for their accommodations at a *Pension* in the vicinity of their training location. When she provided Yussef and Ahmed with their new identity cards she was to retrieve their former identity papers, destroy them, and then have the men moved to a new residence.

CHAPTER 3
PHASE TWO

Samantha met Yussef and Ahmed at the hostel and presented them their new identity cards. She retrieved all the identity papers they had in their possession. There would be nothing kept that would link them to their past. They were now James Frey and Albert Roth. She instructed them to pack their belongings and gave them the address of their new home. Reservations were already made in their new names and they were to proceed at once to settle in. She said that she would meet them at the *Felsen*, location number one, the following day at 10 a.m.

Samantha was at the airport early and met Mary Schneider and Brenda Fischer as they exited the customs area. After a brief welcome, she took them to their new residence. She did not give them their German ID cards, but rather presented them with a self-learning course of the German language. She explained that it was an intensive course and that they would be immersed in the new language, to begin the following day with instruction at a private language institute. They had received some basic instruction in the German language immediately after they were selected for the assignment. Since their intended partners would be speaking German, they were required to speak it. They would be speaking only German from the first day of their schooling and would receive their German ID cards upon successful completion of their course. The second phase of their training would begin as soon as they were connected with their selected partners.

James and Albert were at the appointed *Felsen* location early. The anticipation of their next step had their adrenalin pumping. Samantha arrived and greeted them using their new names, which made them grin. It did sound strange, but they had already accepted the fact that they would never again be addressed by their old names. Their new life had begun. It felt good.

"In the coming weeks you will be learning the location of bird nesting sites. How to identify these locations and how to approach them without disturbing their habitat is important. You will cover this area," she said pointing to the map. "Note the various streams and ponds in this area. Some of these ponds are frequented by migratory birds and some are used as fish hatcheries. Observe and learn. In a short time you will be placing food substances at these locations without being observed. Listen to the sounds of the forest and become familiar with your surroundings. This will be important when you arrive at the mission location." Samantha then instructed James to follow route #3 on the map and proceed to point B. "There you will find further instructions," she said. "Look behind the large chestnut tree facing the cave opening. There are three large stones and your instructions are under the one in the center." She told Albert to take route #6 on the map and proceed to point C, with specific information where he would find further instructions. All instructions were coded. They were constantly being challenged with new information and their capability to follow instructions

While the training continued with James and Albert, Samantha was making preparations for their partners to join them. It was time for the pairing process, and after that, combined training as partners.

***

David closed the files on the second pair of male trainees, Edgard and Amin. They were both Palestinian refugees who had become orphans during the 1982 Israeli invasion of Lebanon. The

French influence that was still felt in Lebanon caused most middle to upper class Lebanese to speak French in addition to Arabic. Lebanon's role as a commercial center, however, made English a must for people in business and it was therefore common for many Lebanese to be fluent in all three languages; that was the case with Edgard and Amin. They would be sent to France for their next phase of training, and it was now time to find matching partners for them.

David sent a message to Natasha for her selection of two female trainees that would fit the profiles of Edgard and Amin. In the meantime, he created new identities for his men. Edgard would become Jean Dupont, and Amin would become Henri Leroux. However with the American spelling, the name would be Henry Lerew. These were the names that would appear on their ID's and their eventual passports.

Natasha once again studied the candidates for a suitable match. Having the profiles of the two men as reference helped her with her selection. Upon completion of her evaluation, she sent the files of two women to David. Hindi and Ashia were well suited to match the profiles of Edgard and Amin. The pairing would once again be David's responsibility. David did not hesitate to accept her selection and immediately created new identities for Hindi and Ashia. Hindi would become Caroline Bardot, and Ashia would become Simone Leboef.

Natasha briefed both girls about what was expected of them. Their air reservations were already made for their travel to Paris. The men would fly separately from the women and they would not have contact with each other until it was time for the match-up. From Paris they would proceed by train to the town of Wissembourg on the German border. Wissembourg, in the province of Alsace-Lorraine, was formerly a possession of

Germany and most people in Alsace (Elsass in German) speak both French and German. This would enable both teams to operate together without any language difficulty. The Vosges mountain range near Wissembourg made a convenient connection to the Palatinate forest of Germany where Samantha could coordinate the activity between the two training camps. Living accommodations were made in a Wissembourg suburb where the trainees were within walking distance of the Vosges- Pfälzerwald mountain range.

***

With some discussion between David and Samantha about the trainees, the match-up for the teams in Germany was decided. Mary Schneider would become the partner of Albert Roth and Brenda Fischer would be partnered with James Frey.

Mary was petite, standing just a bit over five feet. She had brown eyes with Auburn-colored hair that surrounded an oval face. Her perfectly formed teeth shone through full lips when she smiled. She had small buttocks that suited her attractive figure. Albert stood five feet 10 inches tall with brown eyes and black hair. His broad shoulders gave him a stocky appearance for his height. They would make a striking couple.

Brenda was taller than Mary with a height of five feet six inches. Brenda had bluish-green eyes and her hair was dark brown. Her square jaw made her appear serious with a determined and rugged outdoor look. When she chose to smile her expression would change from serious to warm softness. James was an even six feet and he had brown eyes and dark brown hair. He was solidly built and walked erect. The two of them appeared well suited.

The initial attraction was not expected to be a problem for either couple. It was their personalities that were crucial for the relationships to work. Competence in their work was not an issue since they had all proven capable to learn quickly with the ability to apply what they had learned. Now it was time for them to meet. Samantha was ready to make the introductions and note their reactions.

It was not difficult to have Brenda and Mary take a break from their studies to go out for dinner. As Samantha talked with them she was impressed with their ability to converse in German and they were pleased with her reaction to their progress. Then Samantha addressed Mary. "You will have dinner this evening with Albert Roth. I will accompany you to make the introduction and then leave. You are free to spend the entire evening together as you please, however you will return to your *Pension* alone." And to Brenda she said, "You will have dinner with James Frey and I will introduce you. The same conditions apply to you as with Mary. You will not be eating at the same restaurant; therefore I will first take Mary for her rendezvous and then return for you. I trust you will both enjoy your evening. We will talk again tomorrow."

CHAPTER 4
WEAPONS OF REVENGE

While acts of terrorism consistently use some form of explosive device as weapons, a new method of terror was being planned that would be more difficult to detect and harder to prevent.

In July of 2006 it was reported that a deadly virus found in two fish species in the northeastern part of the United States had already spread to two more species. Hundreds of fish in Lake Ontario and the St. Lawrence River died during this period with speculation that the newfound virus was behind the deaths. Three hundred of these dead fish were frozen and sent to scientists at Cornell University for evaluation. The virus, *hemorrhagic septicemia*, was confirmed in these two fish: round gobies and muskellunge. It causes fatal anemia and hemorrhaging in many fish species but posed no threat to humans or other animals according to scientists. Researchers were awaiting test results for the possible presence of the virus in smallmouth bass and burbot while preliminary indications showed that it had spread.

Given that there was no cure for this virus in fish in an ecosystem as large as the Great Lakes Basin, David and his chemists decided that it was an ideal candidate as a virus to be altered so that humans could be infected. Instead of concentrating their efforts on bass or burbot, they would include the trout. Work was in process to create a suitable virus. It looked promising.

The next virus being studied by his research team was for a bird flu suitable for a pandemic. In December 2005 it became apparent that the unstoppable spread of bird flu in Southeast Asia and into Eastern Europe, the H5N1 virus, was one mutation away from having the ability to spread easily from person to person. The threat of a flu pandemic led many governments and public health ministries around the world to make plans.

"Pandemics happen," U.S. Health and Human Services Secretary Mike Leavitt had said. There have been ten in the past 300 years, and "we're overdue and under prepared" for the next one. Would America be ready for a flu pandemic at least as deadly as the one in 1918 that killed roughly 50 million people worldwide, including 500,000 in the USA? David and his scientists didn't think so. The scientists working with David were scientists for hire and worked underground. Knowing the strong arm of the Mossad, they were trusted to keep any work they did secret and confided only to the originator. They were now assigned to work on a deadly virus. Although vaccines were being developed in some countries for known viruses, they would take years to produce. Many countries were stockpiling the antiviral drugs Relenza and Tamiflu, which were thought to be effective in preventing or lessening the impact of the avian flu, but that was not a cure. Furthermore, people had become more vulnerable today than in 1918 because many more now lived in cities that are dependent on food brought in from outside. In a disaster such as an earthquake or hurricane, help can come from outside the region, but with a pandemic, there is no outside.

A World Health Organization (WHO) announcement confirmed the findings of Chinese health officials that a 35-year-old woman who had been working at culling infected birds died January 11, eight days after the appearance of her first symptoms.

The head scientist working for David's group said, "The last flu pandemic, the Hong Kong flu, struck in 1968-69 and killed 1 million people worldwide and 34,000 people in the USA. A strain three times more lethal could kill more than half a million in the USA and send two million people to the hospital."

Armed with this information, bird flu and the fish virus were the ideal candidates for David and his scientists. The initial target would be the northeastern part of the United States. The forests and waterways would be used to begin the infestation of both fish and birds whose virus would be transmitted to millions of Americans. And with no antidote, the devastation would run rampant. Scientists were given one condition. Once they had perfected the deadly virus they must at the same time develop an antidote. The fact that they had an antidote would be kept secret and could possibly be used as leverage at the appropriate time.

***

The restaurants Samantha had chosen were located three blocks apart. She intended to observe from a distance any signs of rejection. Albert was waiting at the entrance of the restaurant as instructed. He watched Samantha and Mary approach and he was pleased at what he saw. The pleasant expression on Mary's face reflected her feelings when she saw Albert. They both appeared enchanted.

Samantha said, "Albert, I present to you Mary Schneider. Mary, this gentleman is Albert Roth."

Albert made a bow, extended his hand, and said, "It is my pleasure Mary."

Mary said, "I'm also delighted to meet you, Albert."

Albert took Mary by the arm and without further conversation, escorted her to their reserved table in a small alcove that offered privacy. He pulled out the chair, and with a slight bow, invited her to sit down. Samantha was pleased at what she saw and departed.

The introduction between Brenda Fischer and James Frey seemed a bit awkward. As a Muslim, James did not have much exposure to women outside of his immediate family and he had never been alone on a date with a girl. He was polite, acknowledged the introduction, but was more reserved. Brenda shared the same inhibitions since she was also a Muslim and had led a protected life before the family tragedy. She had never dated. This was a new experience for her as well. She shook his hand, blushed, and said, "I am most pleased to make your acquaintance."

Samantha said, "I will leave now. I wish you a most pleasant evening."

The training Brenda had just completed included instructions between the opposite sex and how they should conduct themselves – western style. It was one thing to comprehend a situation but another to experience it. Her square jaw may have given her a confident outward appearance, but she was extremely nervous.

The headwaiter led them to their reserved table and pulled out the chair for Brenda, then for James, and handed them their menus. It was appropriate at this point for the waiter to come and ask for their drink order. As Muslims, no alcohol had been consumed in their households, and the thought of it was cause for trepidation. James maintained his appearance and took charge of the situation. He told the waiter that he would have a bottle of Perrier and look at a wine list. Up to this point they had not conversed other than the initial greeting and now James asked Brenda if she would care for some wine with her meal. Brenda smiled and said, "I would be pleased to have whatever you decide."

Samantha returned to the restaurant where Albert and Mary were dining and observed them from the outside. They both wore broad grins and were involved in conversation. It appeared that they were enjoying themselves, and she decided to leave them for the night. She checked in on James and Brenda before retiring for the evening. She couldn't see them from the outside and entered the foyer where she could observe them without being seen. There didn't appear to be much conversation taking place as they concentrated more on the food they were eating. She did notice a bottle of wine on the table and chuckled to herself. It would prove to be an interesting evening.

Albert and Mary were enjoying themselves. It was the first occasion they had to be away from their training and were happy to be dining out. He liked Mary. She responded to his questions without hesitation and always with that beautiful smile. It made him feel like he could say anything to her without fear of rejection. Mary was intrigued with Albert. She liked his mannerisms and noted a peculiar quirk he had when formulating his answers. He would raise an eyebrow, look upward and then directly in her eyes when he responded. It gave her a feeling of sincerity. They avoided talking about their past or their families. Instead they shared impressions of the surrounding area, and when it came to strange customs, their remarks would usually begin with, "Did you notice how…" and then they would laugh.

If Samantha had returned an hour later she would have witnessed an entirely different sight with Brenda and James. After Brenda had finished her glass of wine her composure mellowed appreciatively and she was giggling at something James had said. Her eyes sparkled from the candlelight adding to the warmth of her facial expressions. James had taken the bold step to order wine. He knew he was starting a new life and that he must adapt to the western culture. He also felt it important to take a bold stand, especially with his new partner and was curious how she would react. Since he was no wine connoisseur, he had ordered a local red wine that the waiter had recommended. After he had poured the wine, he raised his glass to hers and said, "To our future."

She said, "To our future."

He noticed how she relaxed after several sips of wine. He too felt more at ease and began to ask her questions about her likes and dislikes in people. He was curious how she viewed Europeans and Americans. Her replies were cautious and well formulated. She was also quick to find amusement in things and her warm personality helped to melt away his inhibitions. Brenda found James to be rather shy, yet when he spoke he did so with authority. She liked him. She knew they had lots in common and that would be revealed with time. Their culture was something they both could deal with in the western world, and they would do it together.

CHAPTER 5
TRAINING ADVANCED

Training was well into its second month when David received a coded message that contained just one word: "Done." He knew the source and a broad smile spread across his normally serious face. He responded at once with an acknowledgement. There was no reason for delay and he could now make plans to move his teams to America. He knew that timing was an important element in any offensive and a sense of urgency was a catalyst that would help drive things to completion. That would begin with Samantha. He sent her a message stating that the mission should be considered to be in an active mode. She knew what this meant. She would accelerate her segment of training and indoctrination. The deadline that David provided was within her capabilities. She would accelerate the training, but not sacrifice important elements crucial to the success of the mission. These elements included psychological conditioning and that would be closely monitored.

Samantha reported the amicable partner-pairing event and David was pleased. It would be important for the new partners to live together for a reasonable period of time before moving them to America. Planning would become critical to insure that enough time elapsed for the teams to be ready and in place to coincide with the migration of birds and the spawning of fish. The desire for vengeance was a constant in the training as well as improving capabilities to carry out the assignment. David knew the importance of mental preparation and he was ready with more material to strengthen their resolve.

Samantha arranged for new accommodations for the couples so they could begin living together. In Europe, living together without being married was common and would not cause anyone to take notice. Once they were settled in their new living quarters, she left them alone for several days while she made preparations to receive them.

***

The same procedures were followed with newly arrived trainees as with the previous ones. Jean Dupont and Henry Lerew were met by Samantha and taken on a hike in the forest to a meeting place that had provisions for their use in training. She provided them with maps of the hiking trails and asked them to familiarize themselves with the geography encompassed by the.map.

Samantha did not work alone. She had a helper to assist with the numerous details of the training process, but was never visible to the trainees. The helper kept the meeting places supplied with provisions, observed, and reported back to Samantha the activities of the trainees. Monitoring their actions helped insure that the trainees were following instructions without deviation.

The following day Samantha met with Caroline Bardot and Simone Leboef who had arrived by train from Paris. There was no need for language instruction as with the first female participants in Germany and they were ready at once to commence their assimilated wilderness exercise in the forest region. Samantha provided them with maps and assigned trails they would use to avoid coming in contact with their future partners until the appropriate time.

There was a sense of excitement for all the trainees with their new surroundings. The contrast from what they were previously accustomed to was enormous. Everything they saw and did was a learning experience and brought them one step closer to their goal.

Adjusting to the new surroundings and circumstances was taken in stride. They were conscious to blend into the society in appearance and mannerisms. There should never be any occasion that would cause them to be remembered once they were gone. Soon forest and streams were no longer foreign to them. They were able to approach wildlife with the stealth of an American Indian, able to perform their work without being surprised by unwanted intruders. Working in pairs became routine with one always functioning as a lookout. The only things they lacked in their training, which would be available to them once they reached America, were handguns.

Samantha was happy and kept David appraised of their progress. It was now time for the second pairing of partners and David sent Samantha his choice. Caroline Bardot would be paired with Jean Dupont while Simone Leboef would be partnered with Henry Lerew.

Simone Leboef and Henry Lerew were both of Palestinian origin. They had lived in the Palestinian territory since birth and frequently witnessed bloodshed. They moved with their families on numerous occasions always seeking a safe place to live. The Israeli push against Arafat caused Israeli tanks to enter the territory and destroy everything in their path. In the case of Simone, tanks crushed her family as they rolled over them. Henry's family were casualties of an Israeli air raid. The sorrow was great but the hatred toward Israel and America even greater. He vowed retaliation and when opportunity presented itself, he volunteered. Simone and Henry had known each other as children in Palestine, but were not aware of each other's involvement in the preparations to attack the enemy.

Caroline Bardot and Jean Dupont were also of Palestinian origin and had lived since birth in a refugee camp in Lebanon. They learned why their parents were living in Lebanon and were constantly reminded of their true home in Palestine. They experienced the frequent attacks of Israeli air raids into Lebanon. After each attack, the resolve of those living in the camp hardened against Israel. It was during the Israeli invasion into Lebanon in 1982 that both their families were wiped out. They were prime candidates for recruitment and needed little encouragement for the mission of revenge.

The pairing began with an evening out as with the previous teams. Observations concluded that the partnership was good. They would begin living and working together within the next two weeks provided that no complications arose that signaled a problem for them becoming a couple and therefore a team.

The team of Mary Schneider with Albert Roth and the team Brenda Fischer with James Frey would both concentrate on fish and birds. Both teams would be sent to New York in the area of Cornell University to blend into the society while they made their preparations for the infestation. They would become familiar with the surrounding lakes and streams as well as locate suitable areas for placing the virus in the nearby forests.

The team of Caroline Bardot with Jean Dupont would be sent to the Atlanta, Georgia area to become familiar with the poultry industry in that region. A person driving through the South might notice the chicken houses dotting the hills and flatlands. One might marvel at the larger ones, as long as a football field. Some of these structures were stuffed with as many as 25,000 chickens each. Since the early 1990s, thousands of chicken houses had cropped up across the South as consumer demand for poultry grew and the U.S. became the world's poultry leader, with production of broilers, turkeys, and eggs valued at $29 billion in 2004, according to the National Chicken Council. Broilers - chickens raised for meat - generated $22 billion of that. The leading broiler production states in 2004 were Georgia, Alabama, and Arkansas, which are home to the world's largest poultry producer, Tyson Foods. That would be their target.

The team of Simone Leboef with Henry Lerew would deal with chickens and water fowl and would be sent to the Carolinas. The Carolinas were deemed to be an ideal location for the virus to infect water fowl.

The Clemson University Animal Diagnostic Center in Columbia, South Carolina had increased its testing for avian flu, including the state's 631 chicken farms, and the state veterinarian's office was hiring extra employees to test at 20 auctions and flea markets where live birds might be sold. The state Natural Resources Department was also engaged in preparing for testing of migrating ducks and other wild birds when they came back to South Carolina in the fall. That plan included getting help from hunters and possibly testing during routine check-ins by hunters at wildlife management areas. Not too far distant in North Carolina, poultry was the single largest agricultural commodity: one of the reasons poultry growers were paying close attention to the slow spread of various avian flu strains in Canada and Asia.

***

David considered the various methods of entry into the USA for his teams. It would be best to take the easier method and use the hard method if the other failed: after all, jumping off a freighter as it entered the New York harbor with someone waiting to pick them up entailed risks of being detected. However, if they succeeded in arriving without detection, it would be easier to get lost in the American society than most any other country. There was no requirement for one to register with the authorities in the area where one chose to live and one could move about freely without notifying the police of a change of address. Entering Canada or Mexico was less of a risk. However, with good identity papers, a direct entry had advantages. The disadvantage was the identity tracking. With a tourist visa they were limited in the duration of their visit and that would eventually cause problems if they failed to depart on time. Entering the USA from Canada or Mexico offered more flexibility.

Rather than risk detection by having everyone enter through the same location, David decided to arrange entry via several locations. Those who would be working in the New York area by Cornell University would enter from Canada. They would carry German passports and fly into Toronto, a popular destination for German tourists. From there they would make their way across the border into New York State. The teams working in the Carolinas would enter the US without deviation carrying Israeli passports, landing in Charlotte, NC. The team covering Georgia would enter the US in Atlanta, also carrying Israeli passports. The passports were authentic in every detail and unlikely to be questioned. They were all arriving as tourists with an American contact and address. The contact names were genuine as were the addresses. Rental of time-share apartments or vacation homes with advance payment secured the address and contact names.

The identities of the teams were known only by a selected few individuals. Outside assistance would be used only in an emergency. An escape plan was drawn up and would be in place if needed. David's American contacts would not be an option since his actions would compromise his own safety.

The final verbal instructions given to each team member before departure were the same: "As soon as you have reached your assigned area, begin at once to assimilate. Avoid any activity that would tend to draw attention to you. Acquire a gun for defensive purposes. Resist any attempt to be taken into custody and always protect the identity and location of other team members."

CHAPTER 6
FLIGHT OF THE FIRST AND SECOND TEAMS

It was a non-stop flight from Frankfurt into Toronto on Air Canada. The economy section of the plane was predominantly tourists and there was a great deal of chatter about Canada and what to expect upon arrival. Mary Schneider and Albert Roth were seated together on a side row with only two seats. Their fascination with every aspect of the flight kept them awake. While others slept they watched the onboard monitor as it traced their route across the Atlantic, past Greenland and into Canada. Living together for the short time before their departure had given them time to get better acquainted. Albert told Mary about his family life in Baghdad, his schooling, his ambitions for the future, and the events that had shattered his dreams. Mary could feel his pain and understood the reasons he had taken the decision to become part of the mission. It helped her to reveal the pain she suffered when her family was killed in an Israeli air raid. The painful death from phosphorus bombs dropped on their home was unforgivable. She often wished she had been home with her family and died with them. She had suffered alone until she was led to the group of other young people whose families ceased to exist.

As the plane approached Toronto, they became apprehensive. It was their first flight to North America and a major step in the progressive realization of their goal. Although every step required caution, it also needed determination to see it through. To play their roles in the character and actions of tourists required boldness and constant awareness.

Albert took Mary's hand and squeezed it lightly. He looked into her eyes with affection. She felt very safe with him and yet she knew that when she entered the customs area of Canada she was on her own. She had prepared herself mentally for any eventuality and felt sure of herself. Albert sensed her confidence and it strengthened his own resolve. They were a team and would support each other throughout the mission.

The plane landed and taxied to the gate without delay. The flight attendant welcomed them to Canada and cautioned them to remain in their seats with their seat belts fastened until the captain had turned off the seatbelt sign. The engines began their wind-down and the seatbelt light went out. Most everyone appeared in a hurry to get their carry-on luggage from the overhead bins and the aisles were immediately filled with passengers waiting to depart the aircraft. An announcement came over the intercom.

"Ladies and Gentlemen. Please be seated. A member of the RCMP will walk through the cabins before you will be permitted to depart the aircraft. For those not familiar with the term, RCMP, it is Canada's national police force. When the RCMP has completed his inspection, we will begin disembarking."

There was immediate chatter among the passengers about the reason for this unusual request. Since they would be going through customs, Albert wondered why the police would need to walk through the aircraft. Mary placed her hand over Albert's and looked at him. Her beautiful white teeth and the dimples in her cheeks were comforting.

Was there a problem associated with them? She thought. *Did someone know about the reason for their trip? No, that was not possible - or was it?*

They could see the RCMP make his way down the other side of the aircraft looking carefully at each passenger. He was obviously looking for someone in particular which could mean that the person posed a threat. When he got to the rear of the aircraft he started up their side of the aisle. He would stop or hesitate and then continue. When he came to where they were seated, he stopped.

"You, sir, please stand up."

Albert's heart was racing. He was about to stand up when the man behind him said, "Are you talking to me?"

The RCMP said, "Yes, I'm talking to you. Please stand up and come with me. Bring your belongings with you."

The man slowly got out of his seat and reached for his bag in the overhead compartment. As they made their way toward the exit, the man's face was flushed and he was perspiring heavily. The quizzical expressions on the faces of the passengers reflected everyone's curiosity about the person being removed.

Albert quickly regained his composure and glanced at Mary who was wiping her brow with her handkerchief while avoiding eye contact with him. A sigh of relief could not be avoided when over the intercom came the announcement that they could now exit the plane.

Having just left Germany, it seemed strange hearing everyone speaking English but it reminded them that they were on a different continent. They got into the line for non-citizens, which moved along quickly. The customs officer smiled and even spoke a few words in German to Mary when he handed back her passport. Albert followed Mary's example and his smile was returned after a cursory glance at his passport and the customs stamp placed on his documents. They then followed the other passengers to the baggage claim. They were carrying nothing that needed to be declared and were not required to open their luggage. As soon as they had collected their bags, they went outside and climbed into a taxi. "Inn on the Park Hotel," said Albert. The taxi driver nodded and moved into the traffic.

Albert had converted some Euros to Canadian and American dollars before departing Frankfurt and was prepared with the proper currency.

"Your first trip to Toronto?" said the driver.

"Yes, it is."

"Business or pleasure?"

"Pleasure."

"You'll like it here. I suppose you already have your itinerary mapped out, eh?"

"Yes, we have planned this trip for quite some time."

"Well, there's a lot to see here in Toronto. You don't want to miss the Harbourfront Centre and the St Lawrence Market. And of course the big attraction here is our own CN Tower. It is the tallest building in the world. On a clear day you can see as far as Niagara Falls."

"Thank you. Those are good suggestions. And we do hope it is a clear day tomorrow. We'd certainly like to see Niagara Falls from the tower."

***

The following day, Brenda Fischer and James Frey arrived in Toronto on Lufthansa Airlines. Since it was a German carrier, the language spoken was primarily German, but the flight attendants were also conversant in English and French. They experienced no problems entering Canada as their documents were all in order. They felt a surge of excitement as they exited the terminal. The sun was shining and their faces seemed to be frozen in a wide grin. They proceeded to the Park Hyatt Hotel by taxi where they had reservations for three days. They had time to unwind and acclimate to the six-hour time difference. James used this time to arrange for their transportation to Cornell University at Ithaca, New York. Instead of renting a car that could be traced, he engaged a limousine with driver that would take them to Niagara Falls. That is where they were scheduled to meet up with Mary and Albert. The night before their departure they had dinner in the hotel dining room. It was quiet with just a few guests and they were seated at a corner table. After ordering their food, Brenda said, "James, you haven't said much of anything about your life in Iraq. I don't want to cause you any pain by discussing your family, but I am curious about your life there. Would you mind very much to tell me something about it?"

"No, of course not. Is there anything in particular you want to know?"

"Nothing specific, but with all the talk about Saddam Hussein, I suppose you were very much restricted."

"Actually not. Before the invasion life was peaceful. It was not always easy with the sanctions that were imposed from the Gulf War, but all the needs of life were available. As long as one did not get involved in politics or criticize the regime, there was no cause to worry.

"You told me that you knew Albert and that you were friends. I know that wasn't his name then, but were there any problems with you associating with a Christian?"

"No. None. Muslims and Christians lived side by side in peace. There were no differences. Christians had the freedom to build churches without fear of persecution from anyone. Saddam wouldn't tolerate it. He ruled with an iron hand. Although there was no freedom to express feelings contrary to the regime, there was peace."

"You and Albert attended the university together, right?"

"Yes, and we had lots of fun. He was like a brother to me. Between studies, there was always a game of some sort to get involved with. We played football at every opportunity."

"Were the studies hard? I hope you don't mind me asking, but did you get good grades?"

"That was a really sore point in everything that happened after the Gulf war. I don't know why it happened, but to get a good grade we had to give the professor a gratuity."

"You mean you had to bribe him to get a good grade?"

"Yes, it became an acceptable practice and everyone had to do it if they wanted to pass."

"What were your plans after graduation?"

"Most everyone I knew wanted a future free of war. They were fed up with the insecurity caused by war and many planned to emigrate to Europe, Australia, Canada, or the USA, or to seek good jobs and a higher education in the Arabian Gulf countries."

They continued their conversation, getting to know each other better until they retired for the evening.

***

Mary and Albert had spent the past two days exploring Toronto and visiting the points of interest suggested by their taxi driver. When they reached the top of the CN Tower, it was a clear day and they could see to Niagara Falls - their destination for the following day. They were enjoying life together. They observed the people wherever they went. A sense of freedom could be felt. And with all the shops, it seemed that anything one would want to buy was available. Most everyone appeared to be affluent although they both knew that was not the case. Still, it was an unusual feeling based on the standards of their country. Another thing that didn't escape their notice was what appeared to be a classless society. It was difficult to make a comparison to Germany since they had not had the time to visit a large German city during their training but had remained in the small village near the forest. They were now becoming familiar with life in a large city in a western democratic country. It was strange, but it felt good. There were no security guards patrolling the streets carrying rifles, as had been the case for Albert in Iraq. The policemen they saw were busy dealing with the heavy traffic and it seemed that everyone had a car.

They sat in a small café with a view of the street. They were curious about everything they saw and wanted to discuss their observations.

"I'm still not clear on how they all seem to have everything they want. How is this possible?" said Mary.

"I read that credit is available to most everyone who has a job, and one can pay back their debts with a small monthly payment over a long period of time. I suppose that allows people to buy many things without having all the money they require," said Albert.

"That's much different from our society. I'm accustomed to buying things only when I have the money to pay for it all at once. The culture here is much different."

They were careful not to express their views where others could hear them, yet they longed to mingle and to communicate with these people. They realized that they must be patient and that the time would come when they could get to know westerners a bit better. However, socializing with anyone would be dangerous and they must be constantly on their guard. It was natural that people would ask them questions, but their new cover would come into play as soon as they were settled into their permanent living quarters. Albert and Mary had become a true couple without inhibitions. The professional relationship they had tried to maintain had succumbed to a basic human emotion - love. Although the love they felt for each other was not declared verbally, it was expressed in action. They repressed any thoughts about a future after the mission. It was the mission that they needed to concentrate on and to which they were committed.

***

Ready for the next segment of their journey, they booked passage on a tour to Niagara Falls. It was a beautiful day and the bus they were traveling on was luxurious with air conditioning. The plan was to meet up with James and Brenda at the Falls on the Canadian side of the border and then go over the border into the United States in the rented limousine that James had arranged. Difficulty in finding accommodations as honeymooners was a normal occurrence at the Falls. They reserved rooms at a bed and breakfast hotel on the American side of the border as an excuse to cross over. Once on the American side they would then proceed to their final destination in Ithaca, New York.

While they waited at the entrance to the Falls for Brenda and James, they familiarized themselves with information about the Falls. It was more than they had expected. They learned that there were actually three falls: the Horseshoe Falls on the Canadian side and American Falls on the American side of the border. The smaller Bridal Veil Falls was also located on the American side separated from the main falls by Luna Island. As they studied their brochures they watched many young newlyweds walking arm in arm, openly showing their affection to each other. That was something new to absorb since a display of affection in public was uncommon in their country.

Albert took Mary's hand in his and mingled with the other tourists. He placed his arm around her waist and she responded by placing her head on his shoulder. Yes, it was a good feeling to be loved and not be afraid to show it even in public. They were so involved in watching the other honeymooners that they didn't notice Brenda and James approach them and were startled when James said,

"Hi, Albert."

Albert turned around and then his face lit up with a smile. He extended his hand to Brenda and she shook it warmly.

James held his hand a bit longer as they peered into each other's eyes. There would always be a basic understanding and reflection of how far they have come since Iraq. They were excited to see one another and decided to enter the restaurant and have something to eat. Although there was good humor between them, Albert sensed that something was not quite right between Brenda and James. Perhaps he was comparing how he and Mary felt about each other and didn't see the same feelings displayed between the two of them. He realized that they were not commanded to fall in love, but rather to work together in harmony to complete the mission. Perhaps, he thought, it was better this way. Should there be problems they could deal with it with more objectivity. On the other hand, it could simply be an outward display of modesty based on their religious upbringing.

They enjoyed a nice meal with chitchat about what they had seen in Toronto and their impressions about the people. There was lots of humor expressed in their tales and it felt good being together. They left the restaurant and made their way to the limousine, still in good humor. The luggage for Alfred and Mary was retrieved from the bus depot and placed into the trunk of the limo. The driver had already been given the address of their hotel on the other side of the border and was aware of the additional two passengers. He had no objections since he was being paid well for the journey and wanted to please in every way.

Crossing the US border was another obstacle to be dealt with, but their apprehensions were hidden. Friendly small talk with the limo driver helped to ease any tensions and appear normal. Remaining calm under stress was much easier to accomplish in a training setting, but this was no exercise. Being in the company of each other helped to sustain a confident appearance.

The driver slowed the Limo and moved in line as they approached the border checkpoint. As it slowly moved forward, they observed the actions of the border guards. In some cases the guard would make a perfunctory glance at the papers and wave the cars through. Other times he would scrutinize the papers and then have the trunk of the car opened for inspection. In one case causing some delay, the papers were taken inside the building for further scrutiny. As each car was waved through they were one car closer to the checkpoint.

They sat quietly with their passports ready. The guard asked for their identity papers and they showed him their German passports.

"The purpose of your visit to America," he asked.

Albert spoke for all, "We are visiting the Falls and our hotel reservations were made on the American side since accommodations on the Canadian side were not available."

"Where will you be staying?"

"We have reservations at the Hanover House Bed & Breakfast on Buffalo Avenue. Our reservations are for one week."

The guard took their passports inside to have them stamped. He returned and said, "Enjoy your stay in America."

The Limo continued on its way. The driver didn't notice the look of relief on the faces of his passengers. Driving over the border to the USA was a common occurrence and he would soon be ready for his next fare.

CHAPTER 7
FLIGHT OF THE THIRD AND FOURTH TEAMS

Teams number three and four left Paris on separate flights. Team number three with Simone Leboef and Henry Lerew were en route to Charlotte, North Carolina while Caroline Bardot and Jean Dupont of Team number four were flying to Atlanta, Georgia. Both teams carried Israeli passports and were expected to clear customs without any problem. Their instructions were similar to those of the first two teams. They were to make their way to their designated place of residence and begin at once to acclimate to their new surroundings. They would speak English at all times and concentrate on learning the nuances of the language in the area where they lived. They would take no action that would draw undue attention to them.

The combined mission of the two southern teams was independent from those in the north. There would be coordination of action but no direct contact between the northern and southern teams to avoid any connection should there be a problem of security.

Samantha arrived at Dulles International Airport outside of Washington, D.C., to begin coordinating the next phase of the operation. She carried a German passport. David was arranging for the transport of the viruses by one of the scientists to a safe location for further preparations once they were ready to begin. The virus for both birds and fish would be sent to Team number one in the vicinity of Cornell University in New York. Tentative plans had been made to send additional bird virus to Team number three whose location was near Duke University in North Carolina, should that be necessary. The virus was being developed to its final stage in the Far East and a small amount would be brought to the US. One of the scientists who developed the virus would come to the US and amplify it fully aware of his own risk.

***

All team members became avid listeners of the daily news. It was not only the local news that was of interest, but international news attracted the most attention as each team member wanted to hear of events affecting their home region. The continued occupation of Iraq and the daily count of the dead were especially of interest to Albert and James and served to reinforce their desire for revenge. Pulling out of Iraq dominated news discussions between the electoral candidates, yet the President refused to admit any wrong doing and wanted to increase funding as well as troop levels. The invasion was now commonly accepted to be a mistake, but the President continued to justify his actions. Many who previously supported him were turning against him and his war. The economy was suffering and the national debt increased daily. To the team members, there was some satisfaction in hearing about these problems, but a slap on the wrists was not enough. They were determined to make retribution. The killing of their loved ones and the thousands of other casualties would be avenged with scores of American deaths.

There were also reports about the search for a negotiated peace between Israel and Palestine. "What a fraud," shouted Henry Lerew. "What negotiated peace. They continue to ignore the fact that they are occupying our territory. What is there to negotiate?

The UN Resolutions are clear. They're just playing games as usual. They continue to talk peace while at the same time they build more settlements. The American government knows all this and just goes along. They conspire with the Israelis, and they will pay for this."

Simone had not said anything. She let Henry unload his frustration and anger, but she was in full agreement. Then she said, "Since the Israelis have taken the position to kill ten Palestinians for every Israeli killed, we always get the short end. But what else can we do? They have American tanks and the best weapons, and what do we have, some rifles and handguns? They even respond with bullets to the children throwing stones at them."

"Yes," said Henry, "but now we will have our revenge. Americans will pay 100 times, perhaps even 1000 times for every Palestinian that was killed by the Israelis."

They were all accustomed to hearing about peace talks, yet they knew that many in the Israeli government were opposed to a peaceful solution. They were familiar with the mediocre attempts made by the American administration for peace that always ended up in failure.

There was one exception. President Carter had tried valiantly to broker peace, but then all the promises Menachem Begin had made to him were broken. The only other time it came close was when it looked like Prime Minister Rabin was committed to make peace. But then an Israeli citizen assassinated him, and the Israelis elected Benjamin Netanyahu, a man opposed to Rabin's peace policy, instead of Rabin's chosen successor, Shimon Peres.

As the teams in the south settled into their new homes they began to learn more about their communities. Religion played a large role in everyday life. There were many Christian fundamentalists in the rural areas and conversations most often turned to religious themes, ideas and views. There appeared to be a great deal of similarity in the devotion of the locals to their religion as it was for the Muslims and their religion. People followed the philosophy they received from the church and it often became political in nature. Often the candidates for president, and which of them would support their religious views, was the subject of conversations. It was these same people who had supported President Bush and helped him win the election. The team members often debated whether Bush was fairly elected. He had lost the popular vote, and then the suspicious voting in the State of Florida where his brother was governor cast a shadow on the results. They felt that Bush was continuing to use devious methods of conduct once he became President. The invasion of Iraq proved his willingness to manipulate public opinion and to manufacture reasons to justify his acts.

"And Bush calls himself a Christian," said Henry. "How can Christians who proclaim to follow the teachings of Christ, discard their values when it comes to Israel?"

"That subject was covered in our training. They told us that Christians were taught that the Jews are the chosen people of God and therefore should be supported. Apparently it doesn't matter if their acts are unjust. It doesn't even matter that Jews don't believe in forgiveness or turning the other cheek as Jesus taught – Allah's blessings upon him! The people turn a blind eye to the injustices inflicted on our people as an accepted practice. The way I see it, using the title of Christian and supporting the crimes of Israel against us is hypocrisy."

"And now they want to treat all Muslims as terrorists," said Henry. "Don't they realize that terrorism started in Israel? I don't think they realize that Israel's own Menachem Begin and Yitzak Shamir were formerly wanted by the British as terrorists with a price on their heads. These same terrorists became Prime Ministers of

Israel and their crimes were overlooked. And now they want to identify all Muslims as terrorists. We fight for our freedom and they label us terrorists."

He turned away in anger and decided to take a walk. It was always good therapy to forget for a while and enjoy life in this new country. Perhaps when his family was avenged he could forget and finally live a life of happiness. The flashback he had to the chilling and systematic murder, one by one, of unarmed Palestinian men, women, and children at the Sabra and Shatila refugee camps was something he would never forget. He had survived and now it was up to him to avenge their deaths. His thoughts turned to Simone. Yes, he could live with her. He would ask her to marry him once this mission was over. Tomorrow he would try to purchase a gun. Getting a hunting rifle or shotgun was no problem, but a handgun would present difficulties. He learned that in South Carolina no permit was required to carry a loaded handgun in the glove compartment of the car. US Law required a background check on the purchaser of the handgun – not the end user.

CHAPTER 8
ACCLIMATING

The first two teams were settled into their apartments in Ithaca enjoying the luxuries of their accommodations with all the modern conveniences. They fought the inclination to think about their future. It must wait until the engagement was completed. There were other drawbacks that prevented them from living normal lives. They couldn't seek employment since they didn't have the necessary documents. The lack of a Social Security card, the absence of a resume with employment history and education, were all factors working against them. They lived at a university but were unable to attend classes without proper records. It was therefore a daily chore to act as though they were students. They purchased books and spent time in the reading areas all the while observing and learning to assimilate. They frequented the local eating establishments and wore the same attire as the other students. It wasn't long before they were engaged in conversations dealing with their faked studies. Seldom were they asked about their origins and they were readily accepted.

The university had a full complement of sporting activities including soccer. In Europe, and most of the rest of the world, soccer was called 'football' - the most popular of team sports. Now they were introduced to American football and wondered why it was called that since the foot was rarely used, but were impressed with its strategy and heavy hitting. There was much to learn and yet the learning was fun. The enthusiasm of the fans and the many expressions used to describe plays or actions was always something new to experience. Everyone had such a carefree attitude about life in general and yet there were those who were engaged in political debates. Listening to the various comments especially when they touched on world affairs was of special interest.

"They are so naïve," said Mary as she and Albert made their way home. "I can't believe they are so ignorant about world affairs. Of course I'm talking mostly about the Middle East region. I just wonder where they get their information."

"Some are just repeating what they hear from home and from the news. But you did hear some rebuttals that suggested they did some research on the matter. They are not all naïve as you suggest. A university is a place of learning and it is healthy that people will voice their opinions. How else will they learn?"

"You're right, of course. It would be good to join in the conversation but I'm afraid our ideas could expose us."

"And how," said Albert. "Our thoughts would be considered so radical that they would pounce on us quickly. And to justify what we say would require us to identify ourselves. We cannot let that happen."

They began hiking in the Finger Lakes mountain region nearby. They acquired a map of bike and hiking trails as well as the waterways. In their efforts to procure a handgun, they learned that the laws in New York State required a license for a handgun but not for a rifle or shotgun. Alfred purchased a shotgun to carry when he went into the wooded areas. He later succeeded in getting a handgun by answering several ads in the newspaper. Used guns of all types were offered for sale. The first two people he contacted wanted complete personal information before a sale could be made. The third person made no mention of ID and handed over the gun when Albert offered cash.

Samantha called Albert and Mary, using the cover name Rover, and said that she was coming into Ithaca and would meet them at their apartment. "Please tell Brenda and James that I will meet with them also. I'll call them from your place."

Brenda and James kept to themselves most of the time except when they were doing combined fieldwork. They would meet together at least once every week to compare observations and to provide any information they thought relevant to all of them. Their mentality was still subject to moods that reflected their Muslim past. It was not possible for them to completely forget their upbringing, and yet their new life required constant work to maintain their composure, especially in the light of news broadcasts. They sought to learn more about Christianity and to observe the lives of those who claimed to be Christians. To their surprise they found that most students didn't attend church and that religion didn't seem to be an important part of their lives, yet each professed to be part of some particular Christian faith or church. They had both associated with Christians in their homeland; however religion was not something they discussed openly. They respected the other person's beliefs, which helped to avoid the possibility of contention.

Here in America they learned about the stigmas toward Muslims. Muslims were most often depicted as terrorists and it was becoming an accepted stereotype. James was not very outspoken, but he felt deeply about his family and his heritage. His resentment toward those depicting all Muslims as terrorists grew as the days went by. They will pay, he thought. If Americans believe all Muslims are terrorists then I shall do my part to help justify their beliefs.

Whereas Albert and Mary tended to mingle with the other students, James and Brenda felt insecure with their new surroundings and would take negative comments about their homeland and their Muslim brothers as a personal affront. While resentment and desire for revenge with them was growing, Albert and Mary were less certain of their rage.

***

Samantha's arrival was met with anticipation. They were pleased with themselves for having come this far without incident and were ready for the next step. Samantha informed them that she had rented an office suite in the suburbs where they would have a place to meet and work. She presented Albert with a bank passbook in the name of Richard Altman and a photo I.D. credit card.

"The address associated with the name Richard Altman is the address of the office," said Samantha. "There is a mini apartment within the office complex that you are free to use. I will begin interviewing some students tomorrow to find the one most suitable for our laboratory work." She handed Albert a sheet of paper. "This is as list of the equipment we need. Purchase them over the Internet using your credit card and have them delivered to the office. Select one of the office rooms that can be used for a small research laboratory and let me know if you need anything else. Okay?"

"Okay," said Albert.

"I will inform Brenda and James of the new office and their responsibilities associated with it. Tomorrow we will all meet at our new office for further discussions. I'm sure there will be questions."

Samantha was gratified with the progress. Everything was moving ahead smoothly with no known problems. She had a good feeling about Albert and Mary and wanted reassurance about James and Brenda before taking the next step. She took in the view of the surrounding neighborhood as she approached their door. It was a quiet residential area with privacy for each apartment complex. Each apartment had a large balcony with a nice view of the mountains nearby. In the winter the mountains were snow-covered and in summer the various shades of green was enchanting. In the fall, the leafy trees stood apart from the evergreens as they changed into crimson colors.

James answered the door and his expression showed his delight when he saw Samantha. "What a wonderful surprise," he said bowing gracefully. "Please come in."

Samantha followed him into the living room. Brenda came forward at once with her hand extended and a sparkle in her eyes saying, "It is so nice to see you again. Please sit down. May I offer you a refreshment?"

"Just a glass of water, thank you," said Samantha. "Have you become accustomed to drinking water out of the faucet or do you still use bottled water?"

"Oh we use the water from the faucet, and it is so convenient. Would you like an ice cube?"

Samantha was amused. "I see you have picked up the habit of using ice cubes with your drinks."

"Yes, it is still a bit odd but we felt it necessary to practice that habit since it is customary here. Excuse me while I get your drink."

"And how do you feel living here in New York, James?"

"Most agreeable. Everything is so clean and of course there are so many conveniences. But I don't suppose that is what you had in mind with your question, is it?"

"Actually it was. I wanted to know if you felt comfortable with your surroundings or if you still felt a bit strange here."

"We have tried to take things in stride and accept things as they are. It was rather stressful at first trying to hide our emotions when new things arose, but we have adjusted to the newness and things don't feel so strange anymore."

"That's good to hear. And how are you and Brenda doing?"

James hesitated momentarily but then said, "There has been no problem living together with Brenda. We get along exceptionally well."

Brenda entered carrying a small tray with the glass of water. A single ice cube and a slice of lemon had been placed over the rim of the glass. Samantha looked pleased and said, "Thank you Brenda. I like a slice of lemon with my drinking water. It makes it so refreshing. I appreciate your thoughtfulness."

"There are some small things that we do miss sometimes, but we have learned so many new things and customs that we now accept as normal."

"How do you feel living together with James," asked Samantha. She could have waited and asked her this question privately, but she was looking for a reaction to the question. Brenda said, "I enjoy living with James. We have so much in common and I feel secure with him." James nodded his assent but remained quiet.

"Is there any reluctance on your part to carry out the mission?" Samantha said, looking carefully into their eyes.

James said, "No, in fact from what I see and hear in the news, I'm looking forward to it. The sooner the better."

Samantha looked at Brenda and said, "I agree with James."

Samantha then told them about the new office and the planned laboratory and that they were entering a new phase. Then she said, "I have placed Albert in charge of the office. He will also be responsible for the supervision of the new employee. He will handle any financial requirements that you may have. This next phase is critical in reaching our goal. Have you secured protection for yourself?"

"No, not yet. So far everyone I contacted required too much personal information."

"If you don't have any success within the next two weeks, let me know. I will obtain a suitable weapon for you. Do you have any questions for me?"

They both shook their heads no. Samantha said, "Tomorrow at 2 p.m. we will meet at the office. I will see you then."

Samantha sensed that the relationship between Brenda and James was not as close as with Albert and Mary. There were most likely inhibitions based on their religious beliefs that played a restraining role, but that was not important as long as they could work together. Samantha would be alert for any signs of discord. She focused on finding the right person for the laboratory. The critical step now was amplifying the virus for the host. Safe handling procedures to carry out the infection of the intended species would be addressed in the final session. If a suitable person could not be found, then David would send someone from Europe to handle the matter. That was not desired. Secrecy was paramount to protect his sources and his involvement as well as those involved in support of the mission.

CHAPTER 9
TARGET AREAS

Preparations to carry out the infestation continued. Identifying the locations where it would take place and the routes to be used with the least risk of detection were carefully studied. Teams one and two worked together in the North while Teams three and four worked together in the South. It was not a straightforward task. Much of the forested areas were privately owned and "No Trespassing" signs dotted the landscape. It was not a deterrent, but required more caution in scouting. At each location, one team functioned as a lookout allowing the other team to approach the intended target areas with less restriction of movement. Bird and deer call whistles were used, when needed, to alert the investigating team of any intruders. The use of firearms would be avoided unless it was required for self-defense. It was necessary for the teams in the South to do more traveling between their respective areas to investigate potential infection sites.

Samantha made frequent visits to all the teams to check on their progress and to resolve any problems. Her activities were becoming more involved and intense as they progressed and David felt the need to provide her with some help. He had considered sending Natasha to assist, but her English was not fluent and her strong accent could bring attention to their operation. Nuances of the English language required time and practice, a luxury they couldn't afford. Mispronunciations or certain choices of words could expose them as outsiders. All team members spoke correct English in an elementary manner. Being at the university made them less conspicuous, but once in the rural areas, they were easy to detect as being foreign.

David decided to involve himself in a more active role. This would also enable him to have more contact with Samantha. The thought of seeing her again caused an automatic feeling of pleasure. When this project is over, he thought, I will ask her to marry me. Thoughts of how they met would always remain with him.

Memories of that event reinforced his decision to undertake the mission that he was now engaged in. He would often visualize the sight and the torture they were inflicting on her when he arrived on the scene. She was a suspect, only a suspect, of engaging in terrorist activity against the State of Israel, and they were using torture as punishment, as though she had been found guilty of the most heinous of crimes. Torture was something that he abhorred, yet he knew that his organization used whatever means they deemed necessary to gain confessions. Her screams and denials went unheeded until he put a stop to it.

The person they were looking for was already in custody and being interrogated at another location. Samantha was innocent and he was furious with his colleagues for the inhumane manner in which they were treating her. She was naked. Tied with her arms and legs spread. They were poking and prodding her with their hands and various devices that emitted electrical shocks. He went into a rage, ordered them out of the room, and demanded a medic. He cut the bindings and then cradled her in his arms until the medic arrived. He made sure that she was hospitalized and treated for her wounds, but he knew that her mental wounds would take a long time to heal. He visited her every day in the hospital.

When she was released he personally drove her to her home in the Palestinian sector and never lost contact with her. It took a long time before she could trust him and accept him as a friend. The hatred and mistrust for the Israeli occupiers was not something easily brushed aside. Daily hardships continued. Did David's act of kindness have an ulterior motive? Could he be different from the others? Why was he doing this? Was it an attempt to alleviate some personal guilt? With time the mistrust turned into trust. Only then did she tell him about other atrocities that caused him mental anguish. His resentment for the organization he served grew until it became irreversible. David remembered the story his grandfather had told him about being tortured by the Nazis. "It must never happen again," his grandfather had said. "We must all work to prevent atrocities like this from happening to anyone." During the 1982 invasion of Lebanon, David's grandfather said that in his childhood he had suffered fear, hunger, and humiliation. And now as a citizen of Israel he said, "I cannot accept the systematic destruction of cities, towns and refugee camps. I cannot accept the cruelty of the bombing, destroying and killing of human beings." When David made the choice and accepted the responsibility to conduct this mission, he made an irrevocable decision to leave his organization and had selected Samantha as his able assistant.

To be near his teams, David devised a plan to open an office in the New England area to represent the interests of the Mossad in that region. When his plan was approved, he flew into Boston, Massachusetts, carrying the virus in small plastic containers, kept cool secured in his luggage. He rented a furnished apartment that would also serve as his workspace and equipped it with the special tools he would need to stay in contact with his office and with the people associated with the mission. At the appropriate time, he planned to send the virus containers to the office in Ithaca for amplification. His location in Boston made him more available to supervise activities in the North so that Samantha could concentrate on the teams in the South. She would personally handle the delivery of the virus to the southern teams thus eliminating the need to set up a separate lab in the South. From now on David would use an alias and the teams would know him as "Thomas Miller."

Samantha was pleased that David would be working more closely with her. She wanted to see him but knew that it would occur only at his invitation. There was always a warm feeling when she heard his voice and a tingling that caused her heart to beat faster. She usually shrugged that off as a being childish, yet it never failed to happen. It was something she had to look forward to but could not let it interfere with her attention to their objective.

Samantha finished her interviews at Ithaca and decided to hire a 23-year-old female Cornell graduate student. The girl, named Joyce, was unattached, and came from a broken home. She was the recipient of educational scholarship grants and stipends that enabled her go to college and she had selected Cornell University. Now she would continue her studies in biological research. Extra spending money was what prompted her to respond to the advertisement that Samantha had placed. When Samantha was satisfied that Joyce had the desired qualifications, she gave her a brief description of the job, saying: "This is a privately funded project that will require hands-on laboratory work. The work is highly sensitive and the person selected will be required to keep all information about the work completely confidential, and of course the pay we offer is very generous. Does this sound like something you could do?"

"It sounds just right for me," said Joyce. "I'd like the opportunity to work on the project and I'm a person that can keep my mouth shut."

Samantha said, "When would you be available to start?"

"I can start at once but not full time, of course. I have my studies to continue and I did understand this was a part-time job."

"Yes, it is part-time. I will let you know my decision tomorrow. But I want to reiterate that you would be expected to treat every aspect of the work as highly confidential. As you probably know, research work is most always done with a high level of secrecy and if there is any public notification, it is normally done after the work is completed. And of course credit can then be given for the role played by participants in the project. Other aspects of this same project may be carried out at a different location. At the appropriate time, the work you have done here will be coordinated with that location."

When Samantha called Joyce the following day with the news of her acceptance, Joyce was thrilled. Samantha informed her that a Richard Altman would contact her with the details about the starting date and her working hours. "Mr. Altman understands that your studies take precedence over this part time work. However, I'm sure you will work with him on any special needs that may occur from time to time," said Samantha.

At a special meeting, Samantha informed the teams in Ithaca that a Thomas Miller would be contacting them to provide further assistance and instructions. There would be a secured line installed so they could talk freely. She said that she would still be available to them should the need arise, but that Mr. Miller would be their main contact from that point forward. She told them that things were going according to plan and that they now had a new employee named Joyce.

"Do your best to avoid contact with Joyce. Albert will let you know what her working hours will be and you will restrict your visits to the office when she is not here. Continue with your preparatory exercises in the surrounding area and be ready to inform Mr. Miller of your recommended target areas. In the meanwhile, find time to relax and mix with the local community as though you belong here."

***

In Georgia, Caroline Bardot and Jean Dupont of Team number four made an effort to become acquainted with a few neighbors and they were welcomed to the community. Caroline fit well into the southern environment with her outgoing personality and ready smile. Jean was also of the same temperament and was easy to like. They had worked hard to develop a pleasing outward appearance to compensate for the sadness within. They were a good match with a common bond and worked well together. At home, they had lived under the same conditions, but in separate Palestinian refugee camps. They were both lucky to have escaped the massacres that took place at the Sabra and Shatela camps where they lived. In the case of Caroline, she had been concealed under rubble and stayed hidden during the slaughter. With Jean, he had been away from the camp roaming the town with a few of his friends when the carnage began. They stayed hidden, helpless to do anything. Afterward, the few survivors had banded together and vowed revenge. It was an opportunity to fulfill that vow when they were selected for the mission.

Caroline and Jean accepted an invitation to attend the local Baptist church one Sunday morning, and after the service they were invited for dinner. They accepted and quickly succumbed to the southern hospitality. Their hosts were naturally curious about where they came from and what they were doing in the local area. Jean told them that they were representing a French company that was interested in exploring possibilities of moving their operations into the local area. "Of course you understand that we are not at liberty to discuss details. Knowing the intentions of the company could cause our competition to place roadblocks in the way. I trust you understand the confidentiality of this."

His explanation appeared to be acceptable and more invitations were to follow. "These are nice people," Caroline said to Jean when they returned home. "They seem to be simple people. I wonder if they have any idea about their government's actions in the Middle East."

"I don't think they care all that much based on their conversation. They are more concerned with matters of the church and things that affect them locally. It would be interesting to get their reaction, though," said Jean.

It wasn't long before they were invited to an outdoor barbecue. "You don't have to bring anything," said their neighbor. "Just come with a healthy appetite. I hope you like chicken," he said with a broad smile. "Southern fried chicken has become world famous and we still make it the old fashioned way."

Caroline and Jean's reaction to this statement was not noticed. Jean thought to himself, They better enjoy the chicken now while they can. I don't think they'll be having many chicken barbecues in the near future.

The outdoor barbecue was a new experience for them and they enjoyed it immensely. The tables were loaded with a variety of southern dishes and everyone ate their fill. The friendly babble continued non-stop and there was always someone with an amusing anecdote that induced laughter. Iced tea was the main beverage and there were soft drinks, but no alcoholic beverages. The hospitality felt genuine. Caroline was a bit troubled about these nice people who were becoming friends. She wondered what would happen to them once they launched their campaign of retribution. She didn't say anything to Jean about her troubled thoughts and didn't know that he too was having similar thoughts.

***

They traveled to South Carolina to meet with Simone and Henry. Henry was busting with energy as usual. He was rather high strung and reacted quickly to any situation while Simone was the opposite in temperament. She was more passive and enjoyed her supportive role. Henry was eager to talk about their adventures and the people they met. After a cup of coffee, Henry began by saying, "I can't believe the people around here have little or no clue of what's happening in the Middle East. They talk a lot about food and the best places to eat where you get the most for your money, but it seems that all their political views are church related. With the upcoming elections, they only wonder which candidate will best support their Christian ideals. Now wait until you hear this. Simone and I were sitting in Denny's restaurant and in the booth next to us sat an elderly couple. We couldn't help but overhear their conversation. The woman was talking about her Sunday school class and about the Israelites' forced exodus from Egypt. And then the lady said, "We may not like the Jews, they reject Jesus as the messiah. But we got to support them. After all, they are God's chosen people." And her husband said, "Well, yes, they have a right to live too. And they have to constantly defend themselves against the Muslims. We got to support them. It's the Christian thing to do."

"Can you believe that?" Henry said. "In the first place there was no forced exodus from Egypt – they wanted to leave! And then to say that the Christian thing to do is to support Judaism and defend them against the Muslims? In their ignorance they are saying that Christians should support crimes against humanity? I don't think they know what they believe nor are they aware of the atrocities being committed. They just follow the line they get from their government and the church. By Allah, would I like to give them a piece of my mind and set them straight on a few things. These people are so naïve and downright ignorant. Sometimes I feel like using my gun on some of them, but I will be patient."

"I think you're right about ignorance and naivety," said Jean. "Caroline and I felt the same way about the people we met. We haven't talked about the Middle East, but we did get the feeling that they were concerned only about things locally. I don't think they really care about what happens outside the borders of their country."

"They are going to find out soon enough," said Henry. "They will wake up fast once we launch our attack. They will learn that it was caused by actions taken by their government outside their borders and it will finally affect them. I don't think Americans have any idea about the horrors caused by their government or the reality of war. They fight wars in a foreign land and their own citizens are immune to the suffering of the people in those countries."

There was an uncomfortable silence after Henry made that comment. In silence they reflected on the actions that caused the deaths of their loved ones. As Jean pondered the act of revenge and why it was needed, he felt that ignorance could not be an excuse to escape blame for the actions of their leaders. "The people must hold their leaders accountable," he said. "That can happen only when the people begin to feel the pain caused by those actions. On the other hand, should these simple people, innocent of any aggressive act, be held responsible for something they are ignorant of? What will be gained by punishing them? Will we feel better about the death of our loved ones because we punished other people? Some of the good people we met may become victims of our actions."

"That is all well and good, Jean," said Henry. "And those thoughts have crossed my mind too. But we have a mission to carry out, and thoughts like these don't help us in any way. Let's not get soft now that we're so close to realizing our goal. They must pay" he said emphatically. "My parents were killed by American actions and America must pay."

Simone and Caroline had not said anything and sat quietly listening to their partners discuss the things that were causing them unrest. When they went into the kitchen to prepare lunch, Caroline asked Simone if she felt the same as Henry.

"I try not to voice an opinion on these issues," she said. "Certainly I think about the innocent people who will suffer, but did they think about the suffering of our people? Did they consider that innocent people would be killed? I believe they called that collateral damage."

"You're right of course," said Caroline. "Getting to know these people was not a good idea. I actually like the Americans I have met. These people are not guilty of any wrongdoing and I must remind myself that they are part of a government that has taken actions that were wrong. If I heard them complain about their government's actions, perhaps I could forgive them. I just don't know how to deal with the fact that they are so naïve and ignorant as Henry said. Is ignorance an excuse?"

"If we were to consider ignorance an excuse, then most everyone would claim ignorance when it was convenient. Did the Jews excuse the Germans who knew nothing about their government's actions? You know they didn't. The Germans paid a heavy price, not just in world opinion, but in money as well. Hundreds of millions of dollars have been paid to the Jews, and they keep going back for more. And whenever it's convenient, they still refer to Germans as Nazis. It's a label they give them because they know how to hate. They will never forgive. It is not in their religion for the Jews to forgive."

"I understand your views, Simone," said Caroline. "But if we take the same position of not forgiving, are we any different?"

"I know what you're saying, but why should it be one-sided? When I think of all the things that have happened to my parents and grandparents, it is difficult for me to forgive. They lost everything they owned. The Israelis took their house and land, and then they took their lives. Don't talk to me about forgiveness. They must pay for their barbaric acts."

CHAPTER 10
ACQUAINTANCES

The teams in the North had not mixed with the local community as had those in the South. Now with time on their hands and being assured that their progress was on target, they decided to follow Samantha's advice and join in the activities taking place at the university and local community. Joining a club seemed a good way to meet people and there were various ones to choose from. Albert and Mary tried to ascertain the purpose of the clubs in making a decision, and that information helped them decide to join the Lions Club. One of the organization's statements of purpose was: *To create and foster a spirit of understanding among the peoples of the world.* There were other community related things that it was involved with, but they wanted to learn what they actually did to foster a spirit of understanding among the people of the world. Since membership was by invitation, Albert investigated the local club's directory for contact names. He selected one at random, a Mr. Arnold Myers, and called him to inquire about the club and its activities.

"Mr. Myers, my name is Richard Altman. My wife and I have recently settled here and thought it would be nice to become more acquainted with the Lions Club. We have studied the purpose of the association and find it interesting and appealing."

"Please call me Arnold. May I call you Richard?"

"Of course."

"I'd be delighted to meet you and discuss our activities and also get to know more about you, Richard. We happen to have a party scheduled for next week and it would be a good time for you to meet the other members. It will be held at the Day's Inn on Tuesday at 7 p.m. Do you think you could make it?"

"Tuesday evening. Just a moment while I check my schedule." He turned to Mary who was listening in on the conversation. She nodded in agreement. He glanced at his appointment book and then said, "Yes, that will be fine, Arnold. We'll see you on Tuesday."

"That's great. I look forward to meeting you and your wife. Until Tuesday then."

"Until Tuesday," said Albert. He hung up.

"It won't be difficult posing as your wife," said Mary smiling. "But I think I might have trouble remembering to call you Richard instead of Albert."

"It is just another test of your ability to retain information. But with that beautiful and smart head on your shoulders, you won't have a problem with that."

"Albert. You always say the nicest things to me."

"I will say even more when this mission is over. But until then, you'll just have to wait," he said grinning. He knew in his heart that he loved her and he could feel that she felt the same way about him. Although they were living together as husband and wife, it was a fraud and he wanted to make it right as soon as the opportunity presented itself. The upcoming meeting at the Lions Club would be interesting indeed.

***

They arrived shortly after 7 p.m. The receptionist asked for their names. Albert said, "Mr. and Mrs. Altman."

"Just a moment, Mr. Altman. I think Arnold Myers is expecting you."

The receptionist excused herself and returned with a man smiling and his hand outstretched.

"Richard," he said. "Welcome. It is a pleasure to meet you. And this lovely person must be Mrs. Altman?"

"Yes, it is," Richard said with a loving glance at Mary.

"Mrs. Altman, it is a pleasure to meet you," said Arnold as he shook her hand. "Please follow me. I'd like to introduce you to our President, Bob Samuels."

After the introductions were made, they were offered a drink and found a place to sit at the table with Arnold and his wife. His wife appeared to be in her 50's, was a blonde with a handsome figure. She looked self-assured and eager to talk. She said how delighted she was to meet them. "Please call me Silvia," she said. Mary felt at ease at once and they began to chat about simple things. Arnold informed Richard about the order and purpose of the meeting that would precede the party. There would be a roll call, introduction of guests, and then a review of activities since the last meeting. There would also be discussions about committees being formed for the various charitable fund raising activities.

"So that I can make a proper introduction, Richard, could you tell me a bit about yourself and your profession?"

"Certainly, however there's not too much to tell, actually. My wife and I just moved into the area and are in the process of setting up an office that will do medical research work. We are not part of the research activities but rather administrators that facilitate research on behalf of other clients. Cornell University offers an excellent back-drop for this activity and access to talent as well."

"You sure picked a good town and a great university," said Arnold. "I'm sure you will do well here and find lots of help. Just don't be afraid to ask if you need anything. But what did you do before you came to Ithaca?"

"An interesting question. I met my wife while studying in England, and after graduation we went to work for a company in Germany as apprentices for this present assignment."

"That's sounds exciting," said Arnold, but before he could pose any more questions, the meeting started. Richard took this time to review what he planned to say. He would be careful to give enough credible information without delving too deeply into details. That was the danger they had been warned about. Seemingly harmless questions could become hazards. Mr. and Mrs. Altman were introduced to the members as guests of Arnold Myers. Richard decided to take the tact of asking questions and divert attention from them. When the meeting was finished they proceeded to the buffet table led by Arnold and his wife. The buffet had a variety of salad dishes along with the main course of fish and chicken.

"At many fast food restaurants you can order fish and chips. Here we prefer to enjoy good trout from the rivers and streams in the area," said Arnold. "Of course chicken is a staple item on most menus. How does our food here compare with that in Germany?"

"I find the diversity of food interesting. What are a bit unusual are the many fast food restaurants. Seems like people want to eat and run," said Richard smiling.

"You're right. People are too much in a hurry to sit down and enjoy a good meal. I prefer a home cooked meal rather than eating out," said Arnold, beaming at his wife. "I'm sure my wife would want me to invite you to our home for one of her specialties."

"Yes, of course," said Silvia with a happy expression. Why not next Friday? Would you be free next Friday evening?"

Richard was a bit surprised at the fast invitation, but turned to Mary and said, "Would that be okay with you?"

"Yes. I would enjoy that.

Of course we will need your address and the time we should arrive," said Richard.

"No problem. Here is my personal card with the address on it. I think 7 p.m. would be good. Is that about right, Silvia?"

"Yes, that's a good time. I shall look forward to it."

"And I'm sure we'll have an interesting evening," said Arnold.

The party activities continued without incident with numerous club members stopping by the table to introduce themselves and extend a welcome. Richard continued to ask questions thus avoiding further inquisition about his background and they left the party early.

***

There was a sense of anticipation and apprehension in the days leading up to the dinner at the Myers residence. Albert and Mary did some role-playing of anticipated questions that would require answers. Making sure the statements they would make agreed with the information they had already given took careful planning. Albert had already learned that the Lions Club had no real presence in Germany and therefore would not likely be a source for information about them or their cover story. In the meanwhile the supplies that were ordered for the office began to arrive and he busied himself installing the equipment and setting up the mini laboratory. Space at a small lab in the city was rented for use by the scientist where he had all the required equipment. He expected everything to be ready within the next two weeks when their new employee was scheduled to begin. He had received a call from Thomas Miller (David's alias) and was told when to expect delivery of the virus and vaccines, which he referred to as "modules." Further instructions would be forthcoming.

Mary and Albert arrived at the Myers residence promptly at 7 pm. Since the use of first names was a common practice, they were greeted as Mary and Richard. Arnold immediately poured a glass of champagne for everyone and proposed a toast to their friendship. "I am delighted to welcome you to our home and hope that we shall become good friends," he said.

"We are honored to be invited into your home," said Richard. He glanced at Mary as they sipped their champagne. Although as Christians they were accustomed to having an occasional drink, they both knew it was important to remain alert.

Until dinner was ready, they engaged in small talk about the neighborhood, the homes, and the status of their neighbors. Richard and Mary were quick to conclude that status was important to Arnold and his wife and that they would be probed more about their profession and family background. During dinner, Richard and Mary kept the discussion centered on food and the cuisine of the region all the while complimenting Silvia on the delicious food. After dinner, Richard led the conversation about the club and asked Arnold what was meant by "To create and foster a spirit of understanding among the peoples of the world."

Arnold laughed jovially and said, "Oh that. Yes, that is one of the statements of purpose that we list. To have a club one must have a purpose, and we do lots of good, as you will learn. It is also a social organization where we get to meet other people of like minds and that can affect business as well. You will find our members patronizing the businesses of each and so forth. But to answer your question about fostering a spirit of understanding among the peoples of the world, I think that is more a personal matter in most cases. There are some people I personally don't care to know, if you know what I mean."

"Actually, I'm not sure I know what you mean," said Richard.

"Well, there are some people who are just plain different in their thinking and their philosophy. They certainly wouldn't fit into our society. For example, I don't think I would have wanted to get to know those commies," he said with a chuckle. "People who are out to destroy our country and our way of life. And I don't think I want to get to know the people who are trying to destroy us now, like the terrorists."

"I like to think that by understanding people of another culture one can find ways to live together in peace," said Richard.

"Yes, those are noble ideas, but I think the reality is different. Take for instance those Muslims. They're terrorists. Their religion seems to support violence and even honors them. When they die, they go to paradise for killing Christians. I don't want to get to know people like that."

Richard maintained his composure and avoided looking at Mary. He said, "I find your comments interesting. Did you ever have the occasion to meet a Muslim?"

"Heavens no! And I don't think I would want to. We live in a Christian nation and want to keep it that way. Then there are all kinds of people around who try to corrupt the minds of our young people. Even here at the university there are problems with radicals trying to impose their ideas on others. We must constantly be alert to stop that nonsense before it gets out of hand. Now I don't mind getting to know people of the world that share our values. There are many people in England, France, and Germany that share our ideals, as you already know. Other eastern countries have been too closely tied associated with communism to change much. Yes, there has been change in Russia but I don't trust them. They're still 'commies' as far as I'm concerned. And then there's China, I won't even go into that. They are communists of the first degree and they are stealing our technology to grow. It won't be long before they will turn on us and make war. Mark my words."

"What do you think about the Middle East," asked Richard. "It seems that each American President has tried to find a peaceful solution between the Palestinians and the Israelis but it never works out."

"I'm glad you brought that up. There is a sore spot if there ever was one. The Jews have always been a problem no matter where they were. That's a fact. They claim the land of Palestine to be theirs and I guess the Bible supports that. And as Christians, we must support what is written in the Bible, don't you agree?"

"It is interesting that you say the Bible supports that view. I have never read that. Perhaps you could point that out to me. It is my understanding that the Jews make that claim in order to take the land away from the Palestinians. The Palestinians have also lived on that land for thousands of years and could make the same claim. I suppose if one wants to make claims about the past, one would have to re-write the maps of the world. The Native American could make the same claim about ownership of America but I doubt that anyone would take that seriously."

"You got that right. This is our land and ours to keep. But getting back to the Israel thing, from what I read, it's the Palestinians that are causing all the problems. Israel is only trying to protect itself from terrorist's acts against them. Isn't that the way you see it?"

"Not exactly, in fact I see it differently. I did some study of that region and learned from people who lived there, and it is an entirely different matter from what you suggest." Richard continued his narrative with a short history of the area. He covered the events that started the problem and where it stands today, and then said, "Don't you think in all fairness, that the UN Resolutions should be enforced against Israel?"

"Of course I do. I had no idea that was not the case. What we get to read here is pretty much one-sided. I guess Jews haven't changed much, as I said before. They sure know how to twist things to make it look like it is always the other guy's fault. I guess that's why, when people want a good attorney to get them out of a jam, they like to hire a Jew. They know all the tricks of the trade," he said with a chuckle. "I'll bet there are a lot of people like me who are not aware of all the facts about the situation there. No wonder there's so much trouble trying to get a peace agreement. With all the Jews in government, you can be sure they have something to do with it. And they put money behind the politicians that support their views you can be sure."

"You've made some good assumptions," said Richard. "I have read about the intimidation of politicians whose careers came to a screeching halt when they spoke out. If one wants to get elected and hold office, they must be careful what they say. There was a recent book written by former President Carter. It is called, **Palestine, Peace not Apartheid**. I read that book and I think it gives a convincing description of the past and present problems. Since Mr. Carter is not running for any political office, he was able to speak freely. I would suggest you read it if you want to learn more about the situation."

"That's a good idea. Silvia, could you write the title of that book down. See if it's available from the library. If not, go ahead and buy a copy. Richard, you know much more about the situation in the Middle East than I do and I appreciate you telling me about it."

They soon turned to other topics, evening came to a close without further information being asked of Richard and Mary, and they agreed to get together again in the near future. When they got into their car to go home, Richard became Albert once again and said, "I think we made some progress tonight. It is amazing to me how ignorant people are about things outside this country. What impressed me was their desire to learn more."

"Yes, I didn't expect that."

"For the club to have a stated purpose: 'Creating a better understanding of peoples of the world,' it doesn't seem to fit the conversation we had. Of course, that goal could have been a serious intention of the club's organizers but the members probably feel otherwise."

"Yes, I had the same thoughts. Did you notice how interested they both were when you began talking about the cause of the problems and the fact that the United States did not support the enforcement of any UN Resolutions against Israel? That was a surprise to them. I thought everyone knew that, but I guess they don't get to hear about those things."

"No, and I think it's mostly political. The Israeli lobby plays a big role and they're always ready with a supply of cash."

CHAPTER 11
DIMINISHED RESOLVE

Samantha got an uneasy feeling after meeting with the teams in the South. The strong sense of determination to inflict punishment on America seemed to have lost its intensity. She tried, in subtle ways, to question the team members about their resolve to complete the assignment and although they had all assured her that they were strongly committed to carrying it out, she felt there was something she was missing. Any weakness or uncertainty with one person could spread and influence others and that could jeopardize the entire mission. She decided to spend more time with them to gain reassurance before reporting her uneasiness to David. She talked with them about the events happening in Middle East and what was being reported in the news.

"The Bush administration is now trying to start peace talks between Israel and the Palestinians. Really amusing, don't you think? Past US Presidents tried and failed for all the same reasons. Now the worst president in American history is going to try his hand at it. Since he was thwarted in his effort to bring a case against Iran so that he could launch another invasion, he now wants to start a new peace initiative. And just as we expected, the moment peace talk's start, Israel launches attacks in the Palestinian territory and starts building settlements again. People are so blind they can't see it. The Israelis don't want peace except on their terms, but they go through the motions as a show. The US gets involved in the peace process to appease the Arab countries and influence world opinion by making it appear that they are serious about peace. And then they want to act as an honest broker. What a fraud. Earlier, Bush supported Prime Minster Olmert when Israel launched attacks against Hizbullah in Lebanon in 2006. That backfired on them. Hizbullah showed amazing strength against a country with sophisticated weapons. Israel lost that battle but she will not stop there. It is just a matter of time. Yes, my friends, what we are planning is just and right. We must avenge the deaths of our loved ones by punishing those responsible. Our people continue to suffer under American supported Israeli aggression and our people continue to die. We will finally bring justice to the perpetrators of these acts in a way they never expect. These people are only concerned about themselves and about making money. They don't care about our people no matter what they say." She slammed her fist on the table and said, "They must be punished."

The reaction to Samantha's comments was positive. She could see the fire in their eyes when she spoke of the deaths and continued injustices suffered by their people. She knew it was important to remind them of the cause and purpose of their being here. Just the thought of how she was unjustly treated and tortured served to strengthen her own resolve. She felt that the mission schedule should be accelerated. She would discuss it with David.

David was having problems of his own. He had heard from his Mossad contact and received reports that concerned his area of activity. He was not privy to top level discussions and learned about these discussions only on a "need to know" basis or from his close associates. He knew that planning to disrupt this latest peace initiative was already in process. He often knew in advance about planned raids into the Palestinian territory and the justification that would follow. He felt disgusted with his job.

He leaned back in his chair and reflected on the manipulation of facts. It was a never-ending process. He knew the ultimate objective was possession of the entire territory of Palestine and that the process to that end was like cutting a piece of salami – one slice at a time. Building the security wall, continuing with building new settlements, constantly setting the stage to acquire more territory under the guise of security. He had long ago placed himself mentally in the shoes of a Palestinian and knew that if he were in their situation he would fight to defend his home. If he lost his home, he would fight to get it back.

But what could be done to change the situation? He knew that the methods used by the Palestinians to retaliate were unproductive – they had tried the same ineffective tactics for almost sixty years – and it only caused more harm to them. To sacrifice themselves with suicide bombing was the ultimate price to pay, but it was a no-win situation. He knew that his country of Israel was strong. She had the backing of the most powerful nation on earth and would eventually succeed unless somehow forced to submit. If she were allowed to succeed, everyone would lose because there would never be peace.

David lit a cigarette – something he did only when deep in thought and trying to solve a problem. He knew that Israel had nuclear weapons that she denied having, and that fact always amused him. Seems everyone knew they existed, but to deny it meant that they would not fall under the various treaties required by other nations. Yes, he thought, deny everything, and cause others to prove it. Standard practice that he was taught. His thoughts turned to Prime Minster Golda Meir and how she had prepared to use the bomb if it appeared that they would lose in the 1967 war. How fortunate for everyone, he thought, that Israel won. To have launched a nuclear missile would not only have been self destruction, but would have brought the Soviets into the picture and may have instigated another world war. Millions of lives were spared. Now the process of giving back the land taken during this war was at the heart of continued negotiations and resolutions all of which meant little to Israel. He had participated in various delaying tactics that would allow more territory to be absorbed by annexation, taking it one slice at a time.

The terrorist's plots against American interests by Al Qaeda were a good diversion; however David's knowledge about all of this caused him considerable unrest.

David put out his cigarette and stood up to stretch. He wanted to rid himself of these thoughts but they wouldn't go away. He often wondered why so little was said about the root cause of terrorist activity. Seldom was it mentioned that it was Bin Laden's frustration over the Palestinian dilemma, and corruption in his own country Saudi Arabia, that caused him to work with the freedom fighters seeking to regain their land. Instead, the focus was placed on any statement, true or concocted, that could be used to infer a universal desire among all Arabs to annihilate Israel or to push them out of Arab lands. The escalation of terrorist's acts simply meant that there were more people available to carry out these missions. He knew that there were those who truly did want Israel eliminated, but they were the extremists.

David rubbed his eyes and returned to his seat. The word "terrorist" was something he knew he would soon become part of with the execution of this mission. At the moment, the label of terrorist was almost exclusively applied to Bin Laden and his sponsored organizations. Why did the world not try to resolve the root problem instead of just concentrating on routing out the terrorist organization? Didn't they realize that Al Qaeda gained popularity among many Arabs for taking a tough stand against Israel and its American ally, thus attracting even more people willing to die for their cause? He knew that this served to help Mossad divert attention away from Israel's subjugation of the Palestinians and turn it to Al Qaeda. He assisted his organization in helping to identify Al Qaeda operatives and provided any information they could obtain concerning planned terrorist activities and disseminate that to the various intelligence services. But now he was doing the planning for an act of retaliation that would be labeled an act of terror. It must be done, he thought. This is the only way to get their attention and resolve the issue. Hitting the heart of America would get the American citizens into the act and they are the ultimate decision makers. Only they could cause the government to take appropriate action. The intimidation of its leaders won't change unless they are forced to change by those who put them into office. That may be the ultimate demonstration of democracy at work.

***

James and Brenda didn't join any club, but they participated in local events. They checked the bulletin boards for activities involving the general public and would make an appearance at these events. There were cultural programs that proved most interesting. Watching the reaction of the audience to a performance by someone from another culture was entertaining in itself. Some faces expressed delight while others showed signs of bewilderment. A group of oriental dancers was featured at one performance they attended and a written interpretation of the dancer's portrayal of ancient customs was provided. Next to James and Brenda sat a man unaccompanied who unashamedly expressed his emotions that others could hear. He found amusement in what he saw and the written interpretation. At the end of the performance he turned to James and Brenda and said, "The oriental culture is interesting, don't you think?"

"Yes, my wife and I find other cultures very interesting. There is much culture presented in this town. I suppose it has a lot to do with the university."

"True. There is always a wide variety of things to do here. After a performance, I always go for a cup of coffee at a small café nearby. Would you and your wife care to join me?"

James looked at Brenda and she consented with a nod. "Yes, we'd love to. My name is James Frey and this is my wife, Brenda."

"My name is Bernard Strauss. You can call me Bernie. Come, follow me."

They walked to a small café located on a side street. Comfortable chairs and tables with tablecloths were intended for the town's people – not the college crowd. After they were seated and had placed their order, Bernie said, "I take it you are affiliated with the university."

"Yes and no. We are associated with a firm that is doing medical research work, and we are here as trainees. I see you are wearing the Star of David. I assume you are Jewish?"

"I'm a Jew and proud of it," he said smiling. "How could I not be?"

"I think everyone should be proud of their heritage and of course many also like to display their religion," said James.

"You are not proud of your religion?" said Bernie.

"Yes, I am, but to me that is a private thing."

To divert any further questions about his religion, James said, "As a Jew I suppose you have strong feelings about the events in the Middle East."

"Strong feelings? I'm not sure that's the right expression. Deep feelings would be more apt."

"What I meant by that is the situation regarding the Israelis and the Palestinians," said James. "I'm curious what Jews in America think and feel about it."

"So you're not from around here I take it. Where do you come from," asked Bernie.

Immediately James realized his mistake but replied in a calm voice, "As I mentioned to you about our affiliation with a research firm, we were sent here from Germany."

"So you're Germans, then?"

"Yes. Is that a problem?"

"Not to me. But to answer your question, you cannot possibly understand how we think and feel. We are a people who have been persecuted many times over the past thousands of years. The Holocaust was the most recent act against our people of which you are certainly aware. Don't you think we have suffered enough?"

"I think that injustice to any people is wrong. The recent suffering of your people was under the hands of a tyrant. The atrocities committed by Hitler became known toward the end of the war. But do you think that two wrongs make a right?"

"What do you mean by that?"

"It seems to me that the Israelis are doing to the Palestinians what has been done to them."

"Hold on there. How can you make such a statement, especially as a German? You should know better to make such an accusation."

"Perhaps through the eyes of a German one can see the situation more clearly, and in school Germans are taught that such persecution could never again be tolerated. And it is not an accusation. There are enough facts to support my statement. Please understand that I'm not making an accusation against Jews. What I'm referring to are the militant Israelis – the Zionist."

Bernie rubbed his chin, bowed his head and then said, "Go on. I'd like to hear what else you have to say."

"The Palestinians are being forced off their land. The hopelessness of the Palestinian people stem from the oppression, murder, torture, mass deportation and stripping of their humanity by the Israeli Government and its forces. It's all true. Incidentally, the mass deportation and refugees it created has destabilized and continues to be a major destabilizing factor in many of the neighboring states."

"Understand something. I'm a Jew," Bernie said. "And as a Jew I support Israel. I may not see or agree with everything they do since I don't live there. All I know is that their survival is threatened and they must fight to defend themselves. I find it hard to believe the things you just said."

"It is all true. Why can't the Israelis just live side by side in peace with the Palestinians?"

"The Palestinians don't want that. They seek the destruction of Israel as their ultimate goal. You know that of course?"

"I think we have all read those things, but I've learned not to believe everything I read. There are always radical elements, usually in the minority, that seek to destroy. But there are also rational people – people like you who are, above all, concerned with their daily lives, with their families and with their future – who sincerely want peace and are willing to compromise so that they can live together. Their voices are seldom heard. Journalism loves sensationalism. Good news doesn't sell. It is the radical views that are more often published and remembered. I think people should realize that terrorism ultimately does not work. German bombings of English civilians did not cause Britain to withdraw from the war, nor did Allied bombings cause an uprise in Germany against Hitler or significantly shorten the war. The bus bombings in Israel have done little to influence Israeli policy, nor has Israeli cruelty to Palestinians caused them to give up. Terrorism tends to strengthen the resolve, and hatred, among its victims."

"You're right about that and I see your point, but I'm not convinced of the sincerity of the Palestinians to live in peace with Israel. I still think they want Israel wiped off the map as stated. Besides which, the land belongs to the Jews who possessed that land for thousands of years."

"It is interesting that you say that. My studies tell me that the Palestinians have also lived on that land for 2000 years. Do you believe it is right for the Jews to want the ancient land back as theirs, yet deny the right of the Palestinians to want their land back also?"

"That seems to be a big point of contention and I can see why there is so much fighting about it," said Bernie.

"Yes, there is. The Palestinians feel unjustly treated. Both sides constantly refer to past injustices and demands for their right to exist. Don't you see that as part of the problem? If they were to forget the ancient past and live in the present, don't you think it would go much better to have peace?"

"Your point is well taken. I am not an historian but I know what I have been taught."

James sat back with a thoughtful look on his face, then said, "Yes, we are all influenced by what we have been taught, and sometimes those views can be a bit prejudiced. In general, it is my view that most people don't hate the Jews but rather the acts of the radicals, the Zionists. They are the ones who have given the Jews a bad name and have engaged in acts of terror. The same thing is happening with the Muslims. Al Qaeda is giving the Muslims a bad name with their acts of terror."

Bernie leaned forward and said, "Well, I don't personally think all Muslims are bad and are terrorists, but you got to admit almost everything you hear about them isn't good. Think of the way they treat their women, for example. Women have no rights whatsoever. And then they punish a woman because she was raped? Come on. That's insane. These people are not normal."

"I read about that too and it certainly hasn't helped their reputation. The only thing I could possibly say in their defense is that their culture and customs are different than those in the West. In the West, we view the rest of the world through our own eyes. That is another problem with trying to impose our ideals on others without understanding their culture. One must keep in mind that every country in the Middle East is different. The thing they have in common is the Arabic language except for Iran whose language is Farsi. In countries like Lebanon and Jordan, women have much more freedom than in Saudi Arabia, for example. And even there it has been changing. Women have much more freedom today than they did just 20 years ago. They have a long way to go before they have the freedom that women in the West enjoy and change will not happen overnight. But that is part of the problem, don't you see that Bernie?"

"You seem to know a lot about the Middle East. Did you live or work there?"

James paused before responding. He tried to remember what an educated German might say and what he had learned at school during his training. He was both scared and exhilarated by the challenge of representing the point of view of his fictional identity. Still, it was so easy to get caught off guard and say something that could cause problems. He could not afford to give the impression that he himself was Arab. He said, "I have studied about that part of the world and have met a number of people from the region. I feel that I have a fair understanding of the area and the religion. That doesn't mean that we must agree with their actions. But I do think trying to understand it is something we should do."

"Have you ever been to Israel?" said Bernie.

"No, I haven't. Have you?"

"No, I must admit I haven't either," said Bernie with a look of amusement. "I suppose when we talk about things from hearsay it can be much different than being there in person. I imagine if I saw with my own eyes what you suggest the Israelis were doing to the Palestinians, I might have a different outlook. I personally don't agree that violence solves anything. That is not to say that all Jews feel the same as I do. We are Americans, you understand, and have strong ties to Israel from a religious point of view."

"I think it's much like politics. If one is a Republican, he or she will vote Republican regardless of the candidate's capabilities or what they have done. The same holds true with the Democrats."

Bernie's head went down. He hesitated for a moment, rubbing his chin, and then said, "For the most part, you're right. Many people will vote the party line. However you will find that many will decide to vote for the best candidate regardless of their party affiliation. And there are also those that will support an independent candidate. That is usually a wasted vote but they try to send a message. But I do get your point. One has the tendency to support one's religion and ignore the imperfections of those who are of the same religious persuasion."

James decided to end the conversation and said, "Bernie, I want to thank you for inviting us and for being so candid. I know I challenged you and expected that you might become angry at my comments. I am impressed with your open-mindedness and your willingness to consider another point of view. I wish I knew how many other Jews saw things as you see them."

"We are all human. We are all uniquely different and yet we still have certain similarities. My wife and I are similar but I married her for the difference," said Bernie with a chuckle. *"Vive la différence!"*

***

The evening had ended pleasantly. James and Brenda discussed the remarks made by Bernie. As Muslims, they knew how their reputation was being tarnished by the radical groups and especially by the Al Qaeda organization. The Palestinian organization Hamas wasn't helping much either. They were the extremist element among Palestinians just as the Zionists were among the Israelis. Bernie was a likeable person and they could see he was a moderate. People like him wouldn't harm anyone, yet his blind support of Israel unwittingly made him party to their actions. No, they wouldn't let this sway them from their mission. Justice would be carried out. Only after that was done would the Americans pay attention. Only when they felt the pain could they possibly understand the pain inflicted on others.

Perhaps a good person like Bernie would be spared, thought Brenda. It is certainly a difficult position to be in. Talking about peace and understanding and at the same time plotting to destroy. I shouldn't call anyone else a hypocrite. *I'm not sure I can do this.*

CHAPTER 12
VIRUS PREPARATION

Albert had been busy. The office was fully equipped and he had arranged for Joyce to start her work. David supplied documents for Joyce to study concerning the procedures to be used. She spent her first day at the office studying the material. Safeguards were included to prevent contamination.

In the field, all teams were conducting studies. The size and number of areas to be infected would determine the total number of virus packets required. Once that data was compiled they could calculate the quantity needed for each location. The plan was to cause infestation simultaneously in all designated places. That was a deviation from the original plan and was still subject to change.

Samantha met with the teams in the South and reviewed the information they presented to her. They had done a good job of identifying potential target areas that met the criteria they had been given. With the statistical information now available she could forward her recommendations to David and await his further instructions.

The teams could sense that their training and preparations would soon be put to the test. They were in position and all they required now were the virus packets with instructions. With time on their hands, they found themselves attracted to local activities. In the Carolinas there were a variety of outdoor recreational activities to engage in. In the Georgia area, high temperatures meant that a lot of sightseeing was done by car or indoors. Caroline and Jean visited the CNN headquarters in Atlanta and took a tour of the Coca Cola plant. Business was associated with every aspect of American life and the pace was fast compared to European and Middle

Eastern standards. Many stores were open every day of the week and some were open 24 hours, an adjustment they were still trying to get used to. It was their perception that people didn't seem to take time for pleasure. They were too engaged in the pursuit of making money that family life didn't seem to play an important role.

They knew that their impressions of American life were influenced by their origins where there was a slower pace of life. The value they placed on family gatherings was not something that was evident here. Perhaps, they thought, the church provided a social arena for family life. However from what they had observed, young people didn't attend church and the social life of the church seemed to center on eating events, like the picnic they had attended. Conversations by many dealt with possessions that they had or recently acquired. Most everyone drove a late-model car. At first they thought that everyone had the money to buy a car outright, as was the custom in their land. Then they heard of the easy credit and that a person only had to worry about making a monthly payment. That same credit system allowed them to buy furniture, clothes, and even a home if they had a steady job. It was possible in this way to have a multitude of material things they didn't own but were making payments on to eventually own them. Caroline and Jean would sit together and discuss the merits of such a system and how they would live in that kind of a society. At first it was exciting to think of having things without having to wait until they had the money to buy them. But it led to an uncomfortable feeling. To have things, using things that they did not own, would require an adjustment in thinking.

"Would you like to live like this?" said Jean.

"I would be happy to live however you chose to live," said Caroline with a smile.

"We would be married of course," said Jean. "And I would need a good job, but without the proper papers I don't know how that would be possible. We could always survive taking odd jobs but that would not allow us credit. And without credit we wouldn't have access to all the things that Americans have."

"I would find work also, Jean. You know that I would want to do my share. But I know you're right. Without the proper papers how could we do it?"

"I think when our duty here is completed we could ask Samantha about getting the proper papers. She provided us with the documents we needed to get here and that means the resources are available to get what we need. If we do a good job, why wouldn't they help us?"

"I think they would. Have you thought at all about the people we will hurt by our actions?" said Caroline.

"I think about it every night lately. But it is something that must be done. We have pledged to avenge our families and we would be doing them a wrong if we didn't carry out this assignment. I just want to do it and get it over with so I can get on with my life, and that means getting on with our life," he said, giving her a kiss on the forehead.

"I must admit that I have also been thinking about it, Jean. I feel so guilty having these thoughts but I just can't help it. The people we have met are innocent of any wrongdoing. They are rather naive, or shall I say, ignorant. They have no idea what their government has done. I think Americans are very patriotic and they want to believe that what their government does is right."

"Yes, I had the same thoughts. You know, I think that too much patriotism can blind a person to reality. A person wants to believe in their leaders and will try to defend their actions. What I find repulsive is how politicians use religion to get what they want. Just by using the name "God" they can do most anything they want and the people will support it. That's where religion can warp the thinking. I have found that in our own country as well. Have you thought about that?"

"Jean. Of course. And I thought it was just me thinking like that. Religion is often used to justify the actions they want to take. In our world, they use the jihad, the struggle, as a holy war to rally people behind their cause whether that cause is just or not. And we know that what they're doing is not in accordance with the Qur'an. I think it is the same everywhere. I was always perplexed in reading history to learn that religion played a major role in most wars. Isn't it strange that people pray to God and ask him to help them defeat their enemies? And at the same time, those enemies are praying to the same God asking the same thing. Does that make any sense?"

"No. It doesn't. That's why I don't want to think about my religion or anyone else's. I want only to think about what is right. I think we all have a conscious that tells us what is right and what is wrong. I would rather listen to that than to the words of a religious leader. After all, they are human just like us. We know that Abraham, Moses, Jesus, and Muhammad were called of God and were prophets. I think everyone else is simply human and guilty of making mistakes, and that includes the Pope. He is elected to that position and doesn't have any special powers."

They continued with their discussion until they retired for the night. Their thoughts were troubling, but they still had a job to do.

***

The next morning they reviewed the areas they had identified for infestation. They also gave priority to those farms with the largest concentration of chickens. The amount of material available to do the job needed calculation. They estimated the amount of time needed to complete the work as well as the hour of the day or the night. There was still a risk of discovery and Jean had acquired a rifle as well as a handgun. The sight of guns was rather common as evidenced by the many pickup trucks with gun racks displayed in the window of the cab. That made the job more dangerous since many of these farm workers, commonly referred to as "rednecks," would resort to using a gun if provoked. Jean began carrying his gun for self-defense purposes. He was an excellent marksman and could react swiftly.

CHAPTER 13
SUSPICIONS

David received two messages within an hour of each other. The first one from Samantha requested a meeting with him. The second, an hour later from Natasha, expressed some urgency to speak with him. David had already responded to Samantha's message asking her to come to Boston. Upon reading Natasha's note, he promptly sent a message to her giving a number to call where they could talk on a secure line. He was puzzled by both messages, but took it in stride. It was not uncommon to wait in this manner, but his curiosity was piqued - especially by the message from Natasha.

When Samantha received his invitation, she instantly booked a flight to Boston and informed David of her arrival time and flight number. She didn't waste any time, thought David grinning. Although there had been no indication of a problem, he was curious about her sudden request to meet with him. He preferred to think about the pleasurable side of her visit, yet was on guard for any trouble. While waiting for Natasha's call, he made accommodation arrangements for Samantha and then reserved a table for dinner at a quiet restaurant ideally suited for romance or privacy. Another message arrived from Natasha saying that she couldn't call him for another day for security reasons. This was disturbing. Still, speculation as to why wouldn't accomplish anything. He resigned himself to wait.

***

Meeting Samantha at the airport was done with caution and the absence of fanfare. They acknowledged each other without conversation. She followed David out of the airport terminal to the parking garage. Only when they were inside the car did David turn to her and say, "Hello Samantha."

There was a sparkle in both of their eyes. He took her hand and kissed it. Then he kissed her on both cheeks in the fashion of the Middle East. Samantha blushed with pleasure at his gallant manner and was speechless. David drove from the airport and entered the tunnel into the city.

"This is the Williams Tunnel, named after Ted Williams a famous baseball player. We are now under the Boston Harbor for the next 3.5 miles."

"Under the harbor? Really?" said Samantha with excitement.

"Yes, and it is also known as 'Big Dig' tunnel. It was quite a project."

It was the first time that Samantha had been to Boston. David pointed things out to her as they drove along. They passed the Charlestown Navy Yard where the USS Constitution is anchored, or as David called it, 'Old Ironsides.'

"The Boston Harbor is also famous for the 'Boston Tea Party' of 1773 that sparked the American Revolution."

"I read all about it but never thought I'd see it," said Samantha.

David's narration was interesting but she found it difficult to concentrate on what he was saying. Instead she noticed his facial expressions as he talked and his calm demeanor. He was an attractive man and she again wondered why he had never married. She was pleased that he was still unattached but she never envisioned anything other than a close friendship. Her love for him was a great deal more than simple friendship. The sexual attraction was, well ... something she tried to hide.

"I've made reservations for dinner. If you would prefer to go to your room first, I can reschedule for a later hour."

"If it's close to the time we can go there now. I'm hungry."

"Good," said David as he turned into the parking lot. "I hope you like seafood. It's always fresh here."

Samantha's expression was one of assurance. "I love seafood. I was actually planning on having some while I was here. How could you have known that I liked seafood?"

"There's a lot I know about you," he said smiling as he got out of the car and hurried around to open the door. He took her arm and they walked into the restaurant. The reserved table was in a small private alcove with beige and brown colored drapes. Soft upholstered furniture and beautiful decorative tablecloth set with two candles gave it an atmosphere of intimacy. A single red rose sat directly in front of her plate.

After they were seated, David ordered a German Riesling white wine.

"This is an excellent wine. I thought perhaps you may have had some while in Germany."

"Yes, I did, and I love it."

"I knew you would."

After the wine was served, he told the waiter he would call him when he was ready to order food. David lifted his glass, held it as Samantha raised hers to his, the glasses clinked, and he said, "To our future."

Samantha was surprised at the toast, but said, "To our future."

David couldn't help but notice the glow on Samantha's face. He always considered her real beauty to be more internal, but he was seeing a new person. She radiated beauty through her eyes. He noticed her small but firm breasts. She did not have the voluptuous body as sex symbols, no; she had the physique of an athlete. He knew she was not only capable of defending herself, but could subdue a much larger person. She was quick and an expert in martial arts. All these things ran through his mind as he pondered his approach. It was time to make a commitment about his life. Samantha had all the qualities he desired. But how did she feel about him? Did she see him only as her boss or was her attention to him more than that? He knew she was grateful to him for having rescued her from the torture, but was gratitude love? Could she love him? He didn't feel there was a problem with his being a Jew and her Muslim. There was never any discussion about that, but might it matter to her in considering a permanent relationship?

David set his glass down, placed his hand over hers, and looked deep into her eyes. The flicker of candlelight caused her eyes to sparkle. She looked as though she were in a trance - mesmerized. Did she feel it? His heart was pounding at the thought of taking her into his arms and kissing her. Her lips were enticing. He noted the rise and fall of her chest as though she was exerting herself in some manner. Is her heart pounding as madly as mine?

"Do you know how much I care about you." he asked.

Samantha's thoughts were in turmoil. She felt something strange was happening but didn't want to misread it. Did he care about her as much as she did about him? Her body was flushed with excitement as she tried to ascertain what would happen next. She held onto her glass to help keep her fingers from trembling. And now he was telling her that he cared about her. She took another sip before she answered.

"I'm not sure I understand your question, David. I know you have cared about me but I sense you are trying to tell me something else."

"I am Samantha. I'm in love with you. I have felt this for a long time but was afraid to tell you how I felt. Are my feelings one-sided?"

Samantha's heart leaped. She felt a tingling sensation all over. The love she had felt had been suppressed for a long time and now she no longer had to hide her feelings. She looked into his eyes and said, "No, David. You're feelings are not one-sided. You must have known how I felt about you, but I had always thought it was one-sided on my part." She continued to look into his eyes and placed her hand over his.

"I love you David. I feel I always have."

Eating dinner seemed mechanical. He had ordered an assorted seafood platter with lobster, crab, shrimp, and salmon filet, but their attention was not on food. It was on each other. The pleasant atmosphere and more toasting made them anxious to leave the restaurant where they could be alone. Foregoing any dessert or aperitif, David asked for the check. He walked her to the car with his arm around her. He opened the door for her and was tempted to kiss her. Instead he closed her door, hurried around into the driver's seat, and drove directly to the hotel. He took her bag and escorted her into the hotel. He waited for her to check in, and then accompanied her to her room. As soon as they were inside he took her into his arms and they became as one.

***

David rose early to go to his office and home. He stood for a few moments looking fondly at Samantha but resisted the temptation to waken her. He wrote a note and slipped out of the room. His thoughts immediately turned to business and the call he was expecting from Natasha. As soon as that was taken care of, he could return to Samantha. He wanted this mission to be completed so he could make a break from his present occupation and start a new life with her.

The call came in shortly after he arrived. He noted the light blinking and then the scrambler activated. He picked up the phone and heard Natasha's voice, "David, are you there?"

"Yes, Natasha. I'm here. Are you okay?"

"I'm okay, but I'm troubled. I think they are suspicious about me and have been making inquiries about my activities. They wanted to know if I was acquainted with you."

"Who made these inquiries?"

"I don't know for sure, but I think it was the Mossad."

"What makes you suspect it's the Mossad?"

"It was the manner in which they conducted themselves. They were not like policemen but acted with more authority, as though they were above the law. They made the usual threats, only worse than before. They seemed to know everything about me, except for my association with you, of course. They suspected I was in some way associated with an underground organization. That's what they were trying to find out. They wanted to know whom I was working for. Did I have any connection with Israel's secret service? They said that without mentioning the name of Mossad. I denied everything. I just thought you should know, David."

"Thanks for calling Natasha. It was important that you did. For the present, do nothing. Conduct yourself routinely but do nothing associated with our endeavor. If they should contact you again, tell them you will go to the police and complain about their harassment. Don't be intimidated. Try to be in the company of someone else at all times. Don't call me again at this number. I will give you a new number for contact. Until then, be very careful."

"I will. Take care of yourself also." She hung up.

David remained sitting with his mind working furiously. Were they on to him? If so, how much did they know? Was there a leak somewhere, and if so, who? If he was suspected of betraying his organization, he knew his fate and it would be carried out without mercy. He must change his method of operation at once in order to protect Samantha and continue to use her to make contact with the eight people in the field. If the mission was compromised, he must protect those people. David was fully alert. His instincts for action, as well as caution, were engaged. He would assume the worst but keep his operational plans in place in case his mission was not compromised. Completing the mission was important to him, but not worth sacrificing his people. He didn't believe the end justified the means if it came to that. That philosophy was not shared by most of his colleagues.

He spent the next two hours trying to locate a suitable office for conducting business related to the mission. Eventually he decided on a small office in Cambridge. He would maintain his present office for work connected with the Mossad but move everything else to his new location. He would avoid doing anything to arouse suspicion. The thought of a surprise visit by the agency and the discovery of evidence about his mission was a risk he could not afford to take. He carefully extracted all materials and disconnected all modes of communication that were non-related to the agency. He packed those materials and called a private delivery service to take them to a secure location. From there he would personally take the materials to his new office. He didn't need to concern himself with transporting the virus since that was held in temperature controlled storage at a secret location. When his office was empty of everything except those things associated with the agency, he did another check to be sure he had removed all traces. Once he was certain that all was in order, he took a taxi to

Samantha's hotel carrying the highly confidential materials with him. On the way he stopped by a drug store and purchased materials to create a disguise. Samantha would need to alter her appearance - especially if she was to be seen with him in public.

Samantha had been awake when David got up in the morning but decided to remain quiet. After the night of lovemaking she knew that she belonged to him forever. Nothing could separate them – nothing. She read the note. *"My dearest, I must leave you for a short while. Get your rest. I will return soon. I love you. David."*

Samantha got up, took a bath, and had breakfast. She couldn't stop smiling. She had never felt like this before. It was wonderful to be in love and to know that the love was mutual. She waited with anticipation for David to return. She wanted things to pick up where they left off the night before, yet she knew that matters concerning the teams needed to be discussed with David and they couldn't be put off. It was the reason I called wanting to see him, she thought. How was I to know that it would turn out this way? Perhaps my concerns about the teams are not warranted.

"David will be the best judge of that," she said out loud. There was a knock on the door. She went to it and asked, "Who is it."

"It's me," said David.

Samantha opened the door with a radiant smile. David dropped his bags and took her in his arms. They kissed with passion. Before things could go too far, he said, "There are some things I need to discuss with you and they need to be discussed now."

Samantha released him and noted the concerned look in his eyes. "There is something wrong, isn't there?"

"Perhaps. Let me fill you in."

When they were seated David told her about the conversation with Natasha. Samantha knew that Natasha was a confidant of David's. Natasha's remarks about her suspicions reminded

Samantha how harsh the organization could be. She was fearful for Natasha and at the same time knew that David was under extreme pressure. His own movements would require more caution from now on. She also knew his responsibility to lead this mission and the people under his care would dominate his thoughts and actions. She couldn't imagine how he had been able to walk the tight rope between being a member of Mossad, working against them, and now leading this mission. That was a feat in itself. The stakes were high. One misstep could be disastrous, especially for him.

As David talked, Samantha wondered if something would happen that would cause her to lose him. That must not happen, her mind screamed. I cannot lose him!

***

At Mossad headquarters a scheduled meeting was underway to review field activities. Reports were discussed and progress was evaluated as usual. Questions posed by agent operatives were answered. Politics affecting the State of Israel was always on the agenda. Any activity, regardless of the source location that was adverse to their cause, was a matter never left unattended. Analysis of peace talk reports and pending initiatives was also tabled for discussion. The unspoken question was always: Did the Mossad organization need to involve itself, in any way, to make adjustments or were things on track? Eventually, as the meeting progressed, it was time for new business and unusual concerns. One operative brought up the suspicion of betrayal. It was only suspicion at this point, but it concerned actions that were being planned against the State of Israel and her American ally.

"What is the source of the information and what do we know as facts," asked the chief.

"The information comes from one of our paid informants in the West Bank. He says there was training conducted in secret, with approximately a dozen persons. He heard that they were being trained to be sent to the west – presumably America. He doesn't know the identity of the persons trained, but Palestinians were among them. He suspects the trainers were connected to people inside Israel. His information was obtained with difficulty since there was a lot of security."

"Where did this training take place?"

"Inside Lebanon near a Palestinian camp. He also reports that there was a second training camp involving females and that the trainer was a woman."

"We need names. We need more than rumors or supposition. Put a close watch on our American operatives. Check to see if there are any inconsistencies in their reporting or actions. I will expect a report by next Monday at the latest. And the suspicion of insider involvement doesn't leave this room. See if the informant can get more information from his contacts in Lebanon. Pay whatever he wants so long as he gets good information. We need names, especially if someone here in Israel is connected with this. For them to operate with such a level of security makes their activities suspect."

"Sir, we have already talked with one female who we regard as suspicious," said the operative. "We didn't learn anything, but we have her under surveillance."

"Good. Apply some pressure if you think it may help loosen her tongue. What made you suspicious of her?"

"She is known to be sympathetic to the Palestinians and has made statements critical of our government."

"Is she an Israeli citizen?"

"Yes. She came from Russia. Her background indicates that she had training in the military and was a candidate for the KGB before immigrating to Israel. We were surprised at her sympathies and strongly suggested that she refrain from any further criticism. There is, however, one other thing that you should know. She was seen in the company of one of our own operatives."

"One of our own?"

"Yes. David Levy. He's currently operating out of Boston."

The chief rubbed his chin. "That's disturbing. His record has been clean to my knowledge, except for one incident where he took exception to the interrogation methods of a suspected terrorist. I also understand he had further contact with that person afterward. Perhaps he has become soft or his sympathies have shifted. Have his movements monitored and check out his office. I will put out an alert to our key operatives of a possible terrorist plot. Alert American Homeland Security as well."

***

When David had finished telling Samantha about the call from Natasha and the suspicions aroused, she felt it was time to inform him about the teams.

"David, I have an uneasy feeling about some of the team members. I sense that their resolve to complete the mission might be wavering."

"Has anyone said anything to make you feel that way?"

"Nothing specific. Comments gleaned from conversations tell me that they have become fond of where they are living and have made friends. That can be a problem if they see those friends as possible victims."

"True. The date for the mission must be moved up. I'll discuss that in more detail with you, but first I need to get my communication equipment organized at a new location. I can use your help, but you require a change in appearance."

David sat down. Taking materials from a special bag, he altered his appearance with expertise.

"You have obviously done this before," said Samantha. "But I prefer the original," She laughed.

"Now it's your turn," he said. She sat down and David applied the right touches to alter her look and gave her a wig that he had just purchased. "The wig is not supposed to enhance your looks but to alter them. I think it does that well," he said with a grin.

They left the hotel and traveled to the Cambridge office by taxi. David used his alias as Thomas Miller and picked up the keys from the rental agent. The new office was small and simply furnished but adequate. He could store his sensitive material and have a facility to connect with his people using secure lines and decoding devices. He was certain he would be under surveillance and monitored as a precaution. Therefore Samantha would resume her visits with the teams in Ithaca, New York. David decided to give Samantha the sealed box containing the virus to take with her. It would be picked up by the scientist waiting at the private lab to start the amplification process. He needed to safeguard her identity, which meant they could not be seen together in public without a disguise.

With the new office set up and operational, Samantha contacted all the team leaders for a status check. She knew that if there were any problems they would tell her. When she had completed her calls, she was satisfied nothing new had developed since her last contact. She promised to be in touch again within a few days. She also gave them a number to call if there was any urgency. If she were not available, they would talk to a Mr. Thomas Miller.

David sent Samantha back to her hotel alone, telling her that he would see her later in the evening. He needed to check in at his home office. Samantha threw her arms around his neck and said, "I'll be waiting."

David took a taxi to a train substation that had lockers. He removed his disguise in the men's room and placed the material in the locker. He then took a taxi to his office appearing as usual. He checked for messages but found nothing new. There were some bulletins from the home office concerning regular business but nothing out of the ordinary. He had submitted his weekly report the day before and therefore had no pressing business. His weekly reports usually consisted of observations about political matters that had reference to the State of Israel. His primary function was planting information that could be picked up by the media. He was also in contact with other public and private organizations that were influential in public opinion. Any negativity that could be detrimental to Israel was dealt with quickly. Intimidation was a carefully crafted art that was used by all agents and the results were almost always effective.

David did a thorough security check of his office apartment. When he was satisfied there had been no security breach or any bugs installed, he laid some traps that would alert him if his office was infiltrated. When that was completed, he showered and changed his clothes for an evening out. He carried with him a small bag with articles needed for changing his appearance. He walked to the subway and took a tram to the station. When he was certain that he had not been followed, he retrieved his material from the locker and entered the men's room and put on the disguise. He placed his change of clothes in the locker, walked out, and hailed a taxi.

Samantha looked through the peephole and didn't recognize the person who had knocked. "Who is it?"

"It's me, Samantha," said David.

She recognized his voice and opened the door. He entered and quickly closed the door taking her in his arms without saying a word. They remained in their embrace for several minutes. The new emotions they felt since their acknowledged love was now impacted with concerns about their mission. Potential problems served to heighten the tension.

They had each other. At the moment that was more important than anything else. The love they felt vanquished all other thoughts as they found themselves in bed succumbing to waves of passion.

CHAPTER 14
ENLIGHTENMENT

Natasha was shadowed everywhere she went. It was deliberate harassment intended to provoke her into making a wrong move. The Mossad didn't need an excuse to interrogate anyone since they operated with impunity, but with Natasha it was different. Her former training, which included the art and style of interrogation, would make it difficult to break her. They would be patient. Sooner or later she would make a false move and that would give them the leverage they needed. The hatred she felt for the Mossad and their tactics deepened. She felt the oppression that others were made to feel who fell victim to their tactics. She knew she was guilty of being part of a planned traitorous and terrorist action, but she justified her participation as necessary to bring about justice and punish the oppressors. Being under surveillance would make it more difficult to communicate with David. Even if they suspected an association with him she must be careful not to do anything that would give them reason to suspect recent contact. It would be the end for both of them and most likely all those associated with the mission.

The Mossad had acted fast, but thanks to the call from Natasha, David was a step ahead of them. When he left his office to go to Samantha, they had immediately gained entry. They were careful not to leave any trace of their intrusion not realizing that David had laid traps. Although they found the office to be clean, they still planted a bug to monitor his calls. The next step was to follow him for a few days and then send their report. Since there were two of them, they could maintain a 24 hour surveillance. The watch would begin when David returned to his office.

***

Rather than flying, Samantha rented a car for her trip to Ithaca, New York, carrying with her the sealed packet of virus. Updated handling instructions that David received from his scientists, along with the procedures to be used in reproduction of the viruses, were also with her. The material would be placed in a refrigerated safe with access by the scientist until it was time for Joyce to perform the work. Samantha wanted to meet once more with each of the teams before final preparations were made to deliver the virus substances. If everything was positive, within a few more weeks the virus would be in a state of readiness for them to begin their work in spreading them in the planned areas. Any further delay would result in failure. Now that the Mossad was suspicious, they would start investigating. If there was anything to be found, they would find it. She feared that it was just a matter of time. She tried not to think about the fate of David if they found him out. If they were able to find one person who was part of the mission, that person would be tortured into revealing the names of others. She knew that David would never reveal the names of anyone regardless of torture, but there may be others who would succumb. Now that she and David had expressed their love for one another, she could not accept living without him. She would do anything to protect him even if it cost her life.

***

When Samantha arrived in Ithaca she immediately met with Albert to discuss activities at the office and to give him the materials she had brought with her. He received his instructions concerning the handling of the viruses and the procedures to follow. He detected a sense of urgency in Samantha's voice as she reviewed the plans with him. Afterward, when she met privately with Albert and Mary, she felt confident that they were still steadfast in their commitment to complete the mission. The level of intensity with the fever for revenge had waned. That was natural, but they wanted the mission to be behind them so that they could start a new life for themselves.

Albert and Mary's meeting with the Lions club and their association with Arnold and Silvia did not appear to have altered their commitment, but it did place questions in their minds. Mary told Albert that she didn't want to meet more new people since it caused her feelings of guilt. Albert did his best to stay focused on his duties. He determined that they should not attend any more functions or accept any new invitations. From now on it was strictly business.

***

James and Brenda were becoming more involved in the community and in meeting more people. Their meeting with Bernie, who they referred to as "Bernie the Jew," caused them much thought. They reviewed the conversation they had with him and had decided to meet more people. They wanted to know more about the feelings Americans had toward the Middle East and especially their feelings about Islam. They realized that what the news reported and what people actually felt and thought could be quite different. The question as to why people felt the way they did was always interesting and revealing.

The event that would change their attitudes was not far off. The university had announced an international educational forum and had invited representatives from universities in Europe and Asia.

There would be presentations made by the various universities and the topics to be discussed were diverse in scope. The public was invited to attend and also to participate in group discussions related to the presentations. The topic that James and Brenda was the most interested in hearing was titled, "Islam in the modern world." To be discussed was "Prejudice and intolerance, aspects of Judaism and Islam, their relation to each other and to Christianity in a Christian land." Dr. Ibrahim of the American University of Cairo would make the presentation.

Many attending this particular presentation were surprised to learn that three religions recognized the same people in the Old Testament and that the three religions went back to Abraham. Dr. Ibrahim explained that the Muslims refer to Jews, Christianity and themselves as "People of the Book," meaning the holy books – the Bible and the Qur'an. He further explained that those three religions are the only ones widely called revealed religions, meaning that God revealed himself to these three.

"You may be interested to learn that even though the Jews don't recognize the New Testament, Islam recognizes Jesus as a prophet, the Qur'an calls him "Isa", and Jesus and Mary are mentioned numerous times in the Qur'an," said Dr. Ibrahim. "Islamic origins go back to Ishmael, the son of Abraham. This connection occurred after Abraham's wife Sarah, bore Isaac. According to the Old Testament, she asked her husband to get rid of Ishmael, Abraham's son that was born by Hagar, his servant. Ishmael and his mother were sent away and they ended up in Arabia. Being near death with nothing to drink, Hagar prayed to God and He told her to dig a well, and water sprang forth. The well is called Zamzam, located near Mecca. It is still revered today when the Muslims go on their Hajj. I think you'll find that Islam shares many elements with Christianity that is not shared with

Judaism. Muhammad is considered a prophet or messenger of God and his words were recorded and became the Qur'an (the Islamic bible). Islam considers Jesus also a prophet whose words, and those of his followers, were written and became the New Testament."

The room was crowded for the group discussion on this subject. Most of what had been presented was new to those in attendance. It served to elicit more questions and to delve into the problems existing today between the Muslims and the Jews. As one participant put it, "If Muslims and the Jews are blood related, why is it so difficult for them to get along? Is it the difference in religious philosophy?"

Dr. Ibrahim smiled and said, "That's an interesting question. Perhaps I could ask a similar question about Christianity and Judaism. Since Jesus was a Jew and Christianity is based on the teachings of Jesus, why have problems existed between the Jews and Christians?

Dr. Ibrahim paused while some members of the audience were discussing the matter, and then continued. "Remember also that the Roman Catholic Church started the Crusades. When they entered Jerusalem in 1099, the crusaders went on a rampage, killing anyone not of their church, including Jews, Muslims, and other, non-Catholic Christians. Don't forget the Christian-on-Christian massacres, which occurred throughout the Middle Ages. When we talk religious philosophy we must remember that the difference in philosophy has caused many wars and is still the most contentious element between the three religions we mentioned, yet all claim to believe in one God. Within each of these religions there are various sects who came into existence due to the interpretation of scriptures. In Christianity there are numerous denominations whose beliefs vary based on their interpretation of the scriptures.

The same is true in Islam where the various sects act in accordance with their beliefs, or their interpretation of the Qur'an. The Jews have similar differences between the Orthodox and the Reformed. As you can see, it is a most complicated situation and the answers are not easy."

"Why is there such a variance with interpretation of the Qur'an?" Shouted a member of the audience.

"When it comes to the Qur'an, what many do not understand is that the Qur'an can only be truly and fully understood in the Arabic language as written in Muhammad's time. Many nuances of the language cannot be accurately translated and this causes much misunderstanding about the meaning of the scriptures. Keep in mind that the word, Islam, means 'surrendering oneself to God.' A Muslim is someone who does that. In this respect, the Muslims regard Abraham as a Muslim as well as Moses and Jesus."

That comment caused some laughter. There was more discussion concerning the subject of Islam but then the conversation turned to the terrorist acts being committed in the name of Allah (God). This was handled with the same calmness as with previous questions. "What is reported in the media is not always based on fact. Hearsay, rumor, and statements designed to mislead are often reported as fact. Ignorance is our worst enemy and that is what education is all about. Learning." said Dr. Ibrahim. "Education is essential if we are to have peace in the world. Greater understanding of one's culture and one's religion is the first step. If we study history we can learn from mistakes, however all too often what we learn from history, is that we haven't learned from history." That statement brought more laughter from the audience.

The meeting ended with much applause. James and Brenda left the forum and were about to make their way home when they spied

Bernie. He saw them about the same time and came toward them with his hand outstretched and smiling.

"Good to see you again," he said.

"The same here," said James.

Brenda shook his hand and said, "Did you enjoy the lecture?"

"Immensely. I was thinking about our conversation as I sat there. It seems there's always something more to learn."

"Yes, it is. I only wish more people could have heard this lecture. Better understanding would certainly help to lessen hostilities."

"I share your wishes. But many are so set in their ways that they don't want to hear anything that could change their way of thinking. I know how stubborn people can be. Would you care for a cup of coffee? Perhaps we could discuss this more?"

"Thank you, but no. I think we'll pass for tonight. Perhaps we can meet again soon. If you will give me your phone number, I will call you."

"That will be fine," said Bernie.

James wrote down Bernie's telephone number, they said good night and went their separate ways. Bernie realized that he failed to get James phone number but didn't feel it was that important. He would just wait for James to call.

James and Mary couldn't wait to be alone to continue the discussion. Their eyes were opened even regarding their own religious beliefs. "Education," said Brenda. "I never thought about it in that way. To educate people about the culture of others and their religion would bring better understanding, and with better understanding there would be less cause for resentment that leads to violence. Don't you agree?"

James thought about what Brenda said, and then replied, "It is true. Still, is that the answer to stop violence? What about those who know better and are just plain greedy regardless of the right or wrong of it? Actions like that have caused violence. How does one stop that? Education is a slow process and is often subject to politics. With the situation as it is, it could happen if there was an effort by the right people to speak out, tell the truth, and then have the courage to do what's right. But I don't think that will happen. There is no easy fix.

"But you do agree that education is the right way, don't you?"

"Yes and no. I'm only thinking of our present situation. How long would we have to wait for things to change? We will take our revenge and hope that it will help solve the problem."

"It will certainly get the attention of many people," said Brenda.

"They may start to ask questions about why it is happening. That has not been the case until now as far as I can tell. People just accept things as they are and think those at the top will solve all the problems. And if things don't affect them personally, they really don't care. They will become educated quickly when events shock them into it."

"I suppose you're right James. I just hope we're doing the right thing."

***

When David returned to his office he knew right away that his office had been entered. The first evidence was opening the door. The strand of horsehair that he had taken from a brush and carefully laid had been brushed aside. The second thing was the position of the chair blocking his desk drawers. It had been moved and the drawers had been opened. Everything appeared to be unmolested yet he knew his office had been thoroughly examined. He next searched for a bug, which he was certain was there.

Without the aid of an electronic detector he would not have found it. He was impressed with their ingenuity in the device as well as in its placement. A bug designed as a paper clip and placed neatly in the paper clip holder was clever indeed.

David performed his routine tasks, made agency related phone calls, and sent emails to other colleagues. Nothing he did within the office would cause suspicion. Next he needed to determine if there was a "tail" placed on him. He left his office unhurried and walked to a coffee shop nearby. Just before entering, he took out a pack of cigarettes. On the back of the pack was a small mirror. When he brought his hand to his mouth to light the cigarette he looked into the mirror and made a mental note of the people behind him. He took a few puffs on his cigarette before putting it out and entered the coffee shop. He found a seat that gave him a good view of the sidewalk. He watched the passers-by and took special note of anyone that appeared to be loitering or just hanging about. He wasn't certain, but he thought he had seen the man now standing on the other side of the street when he had looked in his mirror. That person was purchasing a newspaper at a kiosk. The man got his paper, took a few steps to the side, and began reading the paper. David smiled to himself. Can it be this easy? he thought. Perhaps it is just an innocent person that happened to be behind him and was now trying to get a peek at the headlines. He continued to watch. The man placed the newspaper under his arm and walked to David's side of the street then was lost from view. David took his time finishing his coffee while formulating his next move if he saw the same person when he exited the coffee shop.

When David stepped onto the sidewalk he looked both ways, and then started walking back toward his office. Upon seeing David coming in his direction, the man who had been standing on the corner made his way across the street in the direction of the kiosk.

David continued walking and went directly to his parking garage. He was careful to take note of anyone sitting in parked cars as he approached the garage. He entered the garage and found a place where he could look back without being detected. The man following him had stopped and was talking into a cell phone. David retrieved his car and exited the garage. The man was standing off to the side. As soon as he spied David, his phone went back to his ear. David took a circuitous route that would take him to a mall on the outskirts of Boston. As he proceeded he kept monitoring his rearview mirror to see if there was a tail. He was unable to detect any car that appeared to be a constant in following him. He went to the mall and purchased some toiletries and a few things he may need if he were required to leave in a hurry. He replenished his makeup kit with items useful for more than one identity and then took his time returning to his office apartment. He knew that if there was a pursuer, they would not have been in position to follow him without first making an ID on his car. Assuming that the man he had spotted on foot was following him, he now had the make, model, and color and license number of his car and would be in a position to track him in the future. "Should I change cars?" he wondered. He decided it could wait until later. There was no reason yet for them to be overly suspicious unless somebody had talked, and in that case, they already had information connecting him to the plot. But if that were so, they would have descended on him and he may not have had time to run and could already be in confinement. Fortunately, he thought, Natasha's call put me on the alert. Perhaps they know something and are waiting to see who my collaborators are. He determined to make arrangements for a second rental car that he could pick up quickly. Tomorrow he planned to confirm his being shadowed and then find a way to lose them without arousing suspicion so that he could go to his

Cambridge office location and check for messages and make phone calls.

***

David had a restless night. He thought about Samantha and their love for each other. He thought about the mission and the justification for revenge that got him involved with it. He thought about his collaborators and the trust they had placed in him. What the future would bring was uncertain. Could they carry out the mission without being detected? If so, would they be found out and their lives destroyed? Had they already gone too far to stop? The uncertainties gave him much unrest.

David's main objective the next morning was getting to his Cambridge office undetected. After a coffee and a piece of toast, he checked for messages and then once again laid some traps to see if his office would be re-entered. He walked to the subway keeping alert for any sign of being followed. He didn't notice the man – a different man from the day before, that followed him. As a precaution, David had planned to change trains and then backtrack one station before proceeding to the main station. He took note of those people on the train with him before he got off. He crossed over to the other platform and entered the train going back in the opposite direction. It was then that he noticed a man following him. He suspected it was a tail, but he decided to make another move to test his assumption. He got off the train one stop early and started walking in the direction of the station and the man followed him. David stopped at a kiosk, purchased a paper and then walked across the street to a park bench where he sat, presuming to read. The man following him hesitated, and then crossed the street and sat on a bench farther down the block. David was closer to the subway entrance that was situated directly across the street from him. He only needed to cross the street and then go down a flight of stairs to reach the train. The traffic had stopped at the signal light blocking the road. He made note of the length of time the cars remained stopped before the light changed, and decided to make his move at the next cycle of lights. Just before the light changed to green, David hurried across the street. As he started down the steps to the subway he noticed the man trying to weave his way across the street through the traffic. When David reached the train platform the train was getting ready to move and he jumped on as the doors were closing. He saw the man come running down the steps as the train moved out. David felt relief knowing he had won this bout, but he didn't expect to have such luck in the future. But the faces of the two persons tailing him were firmly etched in his brain.

***

When David reached his Cambridge office there was a message from Samantha waiting for him.

"Dear David, I delivered the material and have talked to both teams. No change from the last visit. I am leaving immediately and going south. I will let you know when I arrive and about the situation there. Please be careful. I love you. Samantha."

He sat for a few moments visualizing their last night together. It would be easy to lapse into reverie about it but he quickly shook it off. He must keep his attention focused on the mission and the problems facing him with the agency.

***

Samantha's first stop was in South Carolina to meet with Simone and Henry. Henry was eager to talk about his progress and to review the target areas he had identified. He spoke with excitement about the regions that dealt with wildlife and his detailed plans to penetrate the farms that raised large quantities of chickens and turkeys. He and Simone had visited these farms in disguise and determined how to gain access to the food supply at feeding time. He was confident that his plan would work. His impatience to proceed with the plan was evident.

"What's the delay?" he asked. "We've done everything in preparation and now we're just sitting around waiting. The last time we met with Jean and Caroline they were completing their preparations. I'm sure they're also ready by now."

"I'm pleased that you're ready," Samantha said. "After I visit with Jean and Caroline I will be in contact with the chief. When he feels the time is right, the mission will commence. You need to be patient a little while longer, but I don't think you have much longer to wait."

"Great. We want to get on with it and get it over with. These people living here in fantasy land have got to pay and pay they will."

Samantha felt assured that their resolve was strong and that there need not be any concern about them. She needed to know if the same was true with Jean and Caroline. Before she left for Georgia, she checked for messages. There was one from David asking her to acquire a message cell-phone. He told her to use only the name "Rover" in her communications once she had the phone. She sent a note to David about her meeting with Simone and Henry and then departed for Georgia. She decided to get the phone in Atlanta where it was more crowded and less conspicuous. She was also looking forward to hearing David's voice again but knew that they would not be able to have an open conversation. She assumed the message cell phone had something to do with problems associated with the agency. Cell phones were not secure and had not been deemed necessary or appropriate in the early stages of the operation. Now with the suspicions by the agency and the surveillance in process together with the mission's launch date being advanced, it may require quick action. At the same time, they would be more exposed. She wished that she could be near David to give some comfort knowing that he was under much pressure on two fronts. The risks they had all taken were very real and turning back was no longer an option. The die was cast and they all had their roles to play. She wanted reassurance that they had full cooperation and participation from all parties.

Caroline had reached a decision. It was not easy to say what she had to say, but she knew it must be said.

"Jean, would you please sit down. I must to talk to you."

"Is there something wrong? Don't you feel well?"

"It's not physical but I don't feel well, or should I say, I don't feel right about what we're planning to do."

"Oh shit. Please don't tell me you're backing out."

"Jean, I love you and want to be with you, but I cannot be party to killing innocent people. I know all the reasons that brought us together and how we wanted to revenge our parents, but I think I would be just as evil and guilty as those who killed them."

"Caroline, I don't want to do it either, but we made a commitment and I feel it is our duty to carry it out."

"You can do it if you want, but I cannot be part of it. If you love me, you will agree to my wishes in this."

Jean bowed his head. He didn't know what to say. He loved Caroline. He also knew that if he forced her against her will, their relationship would suffer and leave scars. He said, "If you don't want to do it, I will accept that. But we need to inform Samantha. I will try to see if there is a way for us both to back out. If not, then I feel I must do it alone."

Jean was in the process of trying to reach Samantha when she called. She arranged for them to meet for dinner at a large restaurant where the noise from many customers would make it difficult to be overheard. It also made it less likely for them to be remembered as having been seen together. They had completed their assignment with a plan to carry out the mission. They too had identified the many chicken farms and the method to be used in contaminating the feed with the virus. Tyson Foods used some of these farms as a supply source and the infection could spread quickly. Their original desire to carry out the infestation however had declined steadily. After their discussion about getting married and continuing to live in America once the mission was completed, the thoughts that dominated their minds changed from revenge to making a new life for themselves. The problem for both of them was having the guilt of causing many deaths and then living among these people. How could they possibly do that? That they couldn't answer. Moving to another area would still not erase the deed from their minds. They were looking for some reassurance from Samantha about their status once the mission was completed and tried to block the guilt from their minds. This meeting with Samantha would inform her of the decision and ask some questions.

Samantha was in possession of her new cell phone but had not yet used it. She looked forward to contacting David after her meeting with Jean and Caroline to give him the number, an update, and to hear his voice.

They were seated at a corner table and started with pleasantries about seeing each other again. Observations about the restaurant, the menu, and the type of people frequenting it kept the conversation moving along. After they had ordered their drinks and food, Samantha asked them about the status of their preparations without reference to the mission. She wanted to keep the conversation in a language of words that would not be understood by anyone eavesdropping. Jean answered in the same generalized manner, assuring Samantha that all was in a state of readiness based on the plan they had previously presented to her. When the food was served and they had started to eat, Jean said, "Caroline and I were wondering what would become of us after?"

Samantha looked at both of them and thought before answering. They had all been told that after the mission was completed they would return to their point of origin unless an extension was wanted or required. Their tickets were roundtrip and their Visas allowed them to stay 90 days. They could apply for visa extensions according to the procedures specified on the card they received from the Immigration and Naturalization Service upon entry into the USA; otherwise they were on their own.

"I think you'll have to be more specific. I'm not sure I understand your question," said Samantha.

"I think before I explain what I mean by that, I must first tell you that I will be acting alone on the assignment," said Jean.

Samantha put down her fork. She sat back in her chair and said, "Please explain what you mean by that."

"It's a bit complicated, but to be brief, Caroline doesn't want to be involved with completing the mis…uh, I mean the project. Also, our time is running out based on the length of stay specified in our documents. Since we don't know when the project will commence or be completed, we were wondering if there were any plans to extend our stay. We also would like to know if it would be possible

THEY PLOTTED REVENGE AGAINST AMERICA

for you to help us with the papers we would need to stay here on a permanent basis."

"You wish to stay here?"

"Yes, if it's possible." Jean looked around to see if anyone was listening, and then said, "We want to get married and stay in America. Of course to live and work here, we would need the proper documents."

Samantha was perplexed. She never anticipated such a question and it was not within her capability or authority to procure such documents. David had arranged those things. And now with him under suspicion, his movements would be monitored and his facility to procure such documents unlikely. Now with this bombshell, just one person involved, it was unlikely that the mission in their area could be carried out. She made sure no one was listening, and then said, "Caroline has made her decision, but I take it that you still want to punish these people that have caused your families to perish and then live side by side with them?"

"Well, that's another thing we wanted to discuss with you. We have come to realize that most of the people in this area have no idea about what is happening in our part of the world. They are ignorant, and in that respect innocent of any personal wrongdoing, and the Qur'an speaks clearly against harming innocents. To punish them for something their leaders have done may not be the right thing to do. If we were to carry out this uh, project, we may be as guilty as those who performed acts against the innocent people of our land. Do you understand what I mean?"

"You used the word 'if.' Have you also changed your mind about completing the project?"

"I have made a commitment to carry out the assignment and I'll honor that commitment. We do however want you to know how we both feel at this point and time. We realize of course, that if we were both to say no, that we could expect no help from you in getting the papers to stay here. That's what makes the decision difficult. You do understand, don't you?"

Samantha looked at Caroline who had sat quietly without commenting. Her head was bowed and she looked embarrassed by what was being discussed. Samantha asked, "Caroline, did Jean express your feelings correctly?"

"Yes. We have discussed all aspects of the situation and what he has told you is correct. I'm very sorry about my reluctance to participate, but I don't think I could live with myself if I was part of it."

Samantha got the attention of the waitress and asked for the check. She needed time to think before commenting further. She informed them that they would leave the restaurant and continue the conversation in the car. She was deeply troubled. This would certainly affect their plans. This team couldn't be counted on to carry out its part of the mission. To think that Jean would try it alone was unacceptable. He needed a lookout and assistance with handling the virus. David must be informed immediately. Actually there wasn't anything further to discuss with them until after she talked with David.

When they reached the car, she said, "I need time to consider what we discussed. I also have a number of things to do yet this evening, so if you'll excuse me, I'll say goodnight and we'll meet again tomorrow. I'll call you in the morning to arrange the time."

***

Samantha reached her hotel and called the Cambridge office number. There was no answer. She hesitated to call his cell phone since that was to be used only in an emergency. She left a brief message that 'Rover' had called and gave him her new cell phone number. She knew he would return her call as soon as he was able to. He was most likely at his office and wouldn't get her message until morning. If he hasn't called by then, she thought, then I'll call his cell phone. She wondered how he would react to the news concerning Caroline and Jean. It would certainly alter the plans. It was too late to activate the backup team. There wouldn't be enough time to get them situated and knowledgeable of the target areas before time would run out on the Visas of the other teams and that could jeopardize their safety, if not the mission itself.

***

David had decided to stay at his office apartment the entire day. He didn't want his trackers to know he was wise to them. Perhaps they wouldn't consider his movements of the day before as suspicious, but simply that they lost him due to a fluke of timing. Another situation like yesterday would tip them off though, that was certain.

Meanwhile, the Mossad surveillance team reported that they had the subject under surveillance and that there was nothing unusual to report. The search of his office had not revealed anything out of the ordinary.

In Tel Aviv there was a meeting in process discussing the follow-up report of the informant. The informant said that those involved in the training, instructors and trainees, were no longer in the area and it was believed that they had left the country. He was not able to locate anyone who knew of their whereabouts.

"Okay," said the chief. "Let's see if I got this straight. We know that training took place in Lebanon. Some of the suspects are believed to be of Palestinian origin. Females were also being trained. Both male and female trainers were involved. It is believed that there is a connection inside Israel. It is suspected that they were training for a mission to the west – possibly America. And now we learn that they have virtually disappeared. Have I missed anything?"

"No, sir. I think that's what we know at this time. We have our operative in Boston under surveillance but nothing out of the ordinary has been detected so far. We are trying to find out if there were any unusual departures from Lebanon by air that would appear suspicious."

"What about the female suspect you have under surveillance here? Have you learned anything more from her?"

"No, sir."

"You said that she had some contact with our David Levy. Have you questioned her about that?"

"Not as yet, sir. Since we started our surveillance she has not done anything that would give us cause to pick her up for questioning."

"Since when do you need a cause? I suggest you pick her up and find out what her connection is, or has been, with David Levy. If there is a connection, we need to find out what it is and bring him in for questioning as well."

CHAPTER 15
SOMETHING FISHY

In Ithaca, New York, Arnold Myers was trying to locate Richard Altman. He wanted to invite him to more club activities in preparation for an invitation to membership and act as his sponsor. There was no number listed for Richard in the phone directory and he couldn't locate an address. He checked new business listings but that also drew a blank. He remembered Richard telling him something about medical research work but that it was rather hush-hush, however it seemed to him there was some connection with the university. He checked at the university but they had no records of any Richard Altman nor did they have any affiliation with a local research company. Nothing checked out. He tried remembering the first contact concerning the Lions club, or anything in their conversation at the club party and then at their dinner together. He realized that he didn't have an address for Richard or even a phone number. There was no way to contact him. That seemed very odd. He and his wife supposedly came from Germany on assignment with a German firm. How could they possibly be here and yet find no trace of them? Something's fishy about this, thought Arnold. And then he remembered the conversation about Muslims and the Middle East. What was that all about? What are they really doing here? He would continue to search for them. They had to be somewhere and he had a few questions for them. I will get to the bottom of this, he thought.

***

Albert spent more time at the office and was becoming more accustomed to his alias as Richard Altman. Joyce referred to him as "Mr. Altman." He did not at any time ask her to call him Richard and succumb to the first name familiarity, as was custom in America, but maintained the more formal relationship between boss and employee as practiced in Europe and the Middle East. Keeping some distance from the employee also prevented questions of a more personal nature. Joyce had performed her work according to the instructions given to her and she was now ready to proceed to the next phase. She assumed that what she had done so far was just one step in a continuing process; however, the virus was now actually in the desired state of readiness. The next step would be to amplify it in the quantities specified. Richard was waiting for instructions on how to proceed. He gave Joyce some time off, citing delays in procedures for the next phase. When he left the office he became Albert once again. He met with Mary for dinner and as usual, their conversation turned to the aftermath of what they were about to do. Innocent people dominated their thoughts. Just walking around the university and seeing all these young people in their pursuit of a higher education made it difficult for them to contemplate the result of the actions they would be taking. In their last meeting with James and Brenda, James told them about the international forum they had attended. The excitement in both their voices as they related the topics discussed and what they had learned was genuine. They believed that education was the solution to lasting peace. The more they talked, the greater was the uneasiness they felt about the mission. They knew that time was running out, and the order to carry out the mission was near at hand.

***

In Boston, David was up early and left his home to go jogging. His surveillance was not prepared for that and it wasn't long before David lost him. When he was satisfied that he was alone, he made his way to the Cambridge office. As soon as he saw the message from Samantha he called her. She answered the phone citing the number. David recognized her voice and said, "Good morning, Rover."

"Good morning. It's so good to hear your voice. I was wondering how long it would take for you to get my message."

"Actually, I got it just a few minutes ago. What's up?"

"We have a problem with Team #4. She filled him in on her conversation with the team the night before and then said, "Jean says that he is still willing to carry out their assignment, primarily because of his promise to do so, but I don't think he can be depended on should any problems arise. Besides, I don't think he can do it alone."

David said, "I agree. This does pose a problem. Time is against us for changing that team. From this point forward, keep them in the dark concerning our plans and try to prevent them from talking with Team #3. Use whatever excuse you need but we need to isolate them."

"Okay. I'll do that. Concerning their questions about remaining here. What do you suggest?"

"Once they are isolated, tell them to use their return ticket before the duration of their stay expires. Since there is no date for the mission to commence, they need to adhere to the legal status of their stay. Papers for proper entry and request for normal immigration would need to be prepared and that will take time. They either do that or they would be on their own and be considered illegal aliens. That would place them in jeopardy of discovery and deportation. Either way, they will need to remain quiet. Keep me informed if there is a problem. And, how are you?"

"Lonely without you."

"Me, too. If it were possible, I would ask you to come tomorrow but that isn't possible just now. I'm under surveillance and must watch every step."

"Please be careful. You are now my life. I want to be with you."

"You will be just as soon as I can arrange it."

They said goodbye but both were troubled. Samantha was worried about David. The mission had brought them together but carrying out the mission was no longer important to her. She would willingly do whatever David asked of her and knew that the risks were high.

David felt that immediate action was needed before things would begin to unravel. That night he studied the target areas and the calculated virus requirements. He then subtracted the requirement stipulated for Team #4. There was just ten days remaining before the first two teams would be in violation of their stay as stipulated in their visas. For Teams #3 and #4, it was just a few days longer. Tomorrow he would give the order to finalize the preparation of the virus packets. Fortunately, the time normally required for this process was foreseen and the scientist had already started the process. As soon as all the work was completed, David would direct the distribution to the teams with the exception of Team #4, and set the date to commence.

CHAPTER 16
INTERROGATION

The knocking at the door continued until Natasha opened it. Two men pushed their way inside. "Get your coat and come with us," they demanded.

"What's the reason for this intrusion? Who are you?"

"Security. We have some questions to ask and you must come with us."

"Why can't you ask your questions here?"

"Someone else will be asking the questions. You are to come with us."

"I would like to see some identification."

Without a response, they grabbed her arms and forcibly took her to the waiting car. She was shoved inside and they sped away. Her mother was returning from the store when she saw Natasha being pushed into the car. She ran after the car screaming for them to stop, but knew that was useless. She immediately reported the abduction to the police. They took her statement and said they would investigate.

Natasha was blindfolded once inside the car and her hands were cuffed. "Why are you doing this?" she screamed. "Who are you?"

They said nothing and continued driving until they reached their destination. She was led blindfolded into a building and down a long hallway. They stopped and knocked on a door. It was opened and they entered. Without any word being spoken, she was placed in a chair, her hands and feet were tied to it, and then they left the room. She presumed she was alone. From her past experience, everything that had happened so far gave her reason to suspect that she was about to be interrogated. She immediately did some mind gymnastics causing her to relax. The isolation technique was just one of many that were designed get the person off balance. Sudden loud noises or strange sounds for disorientation were part of the process. She knew many of the preliminary methods but they would be mild compared to advanced techniques.

In her mind she went on a trip to her birthplace. She remembered herself as a little girl running through the fields in the countryside. She remembered her childhood friends and the fun they had together. There were chores and much hard work but her parents were kind and understanding. They often tried to lighten the load for her. She was a good student, being especially talented with a quick mind. Learning was easy and fun. The future looked bright and she advanced quickly, until the day they turned against her simply because she was a Jew. The trip to Israel with her parents had been filled with excitement and anticipation of a new life filled with happiness, but then that dream was shattered. Now she expected to endure the same fate at the hands of the security police, as she would have expected in Russia. She bit her lip. Her face took on a determined look. No, she would not give them what they want and they would not break her. Without her knowing it, someone had been sitting in the room observing her. She was startled when the person said, "How did you come to know David Levy?"

"Who's to say I know David Levy?"

"Are you denying it?"

"I simply want to know who is saying that I know him. And why was I abducted?"

"I'm asking the questions. You will answer them."

"I am not required to answer any of your questions. You have kidnapped me and brought me here by force. And why must I remain blindfolded. Are you afraid to show your face?"

"I ask you again, how do you know David Levy?"

"Why do you want to know?"

"You impertinent sow." He slapped her across the face. Her head snapped back like whiplash. The stinging of the slap was nothing compared to the fury she felt. If only I could get my hands on that person, he would never slap me again, she thought. She determined to bide her time until she had opportunity to make him pay. If nothing else, the mission will be an equalizer of sorts. But they won't get any information out of me.

"Are you ready to talk? Now answer my question." he said.

Natasha sat silent without any movement. She knew the process. If she answered one question, that would open the door for more questions and it would continue until they were satisfied that they got all that they could. And then, they would dispose of her in any manner they desired. She heard the door open and close. She didn't know if someone had entered or if the person had left the room. She waited. It was tiring not knowing what was going on and trying to guess what would happen next, but she refused to let them see how weary she was becoming. She would remain strong – show no weakness. Then she heard some movement, and then the voice.

"My name is Alan. I just got here. I don't know what my colleague said to you, but whatever it was, we'll start from the beginning. Okay?"

"Why am I here," she asked.

"We have some questions for you, and when we have the answers, we will take you home."

The tone of his voice was pleasant. This must be the bad guy, good guy routine, she thought. Then he repeated the question his colleague had asked.

"How do you know David Levy?"

"If all you want to do is ask me a few questions, why was I abducted and brought here? I'm an Israeli citizen and my rights have been violated. I demand to see a lawyer."

"You were not abducted and you don't need a lawyer. Why won't you answer a simple question?"

"If I wasn't abducted, then why was I forced to come here and blindfolded?"

"If I remove the blindfold, will you answer my question?"

"If I answer your question, will I be permitted to leave?"

"If the question is answered satisfactorily, you will be free to go."

"And if you don't like my answer, what happens then?"

They continued to spar. With every question put to her, she asked another in return. The frustration became evident as the calmness in the voice of the interrogator changed to irritation and eventually to anger. He left the room and she was left sitting where she was. As time went by she became very tired and could no longer sit up straight. When she leaned to the side the cords binding her hands tightened, cutting off the circulation. Her head was bowed forward with chin on her chest. She continued to use mind control to relax and fight the weariness but it was an ongoing struggle to remain upright. She tested the chair to see if was attached to the floor. It wasn't. With a thrust sideways the chair overturned, leaving her lying on her side. That was a relief from the upright position and she felt that she could rest in this manner, but that was not to be. As soon as the chair tipped over the door opened and someone entered the room and lifted the chair to its upright position.

"Are you ready to talk?"

Natasha didn't reply. She heard the man move a chair and presumably sit down in front of her. She was thirsty but would not ask for a drink. That would indicate weakness and they would bargain with her for the drink.

"Natasha. We know that you are acquainted with David Levy. You haven't denied that fact. We wish to know what your association is with him. How did you get to know him? These are questions that require answers. I'm going to remove your blindfold, and when I do, I expect you to answer my questions."

The blindfold was removed. Natasha opened her eyes slowly. The room was dimly lit and her eyes adjusted quickly. The man sat directly in front of her watching intently. He was of medium build with sandy colored hair and he wore a mustache. His eyes were blue and piercing. A notebook lay balanced on one knee. He crossed his arms and said, "Well? Are you ready to talk?"

Natasha looked him steadily in the eyes without wavering, and said, "I am an Israeli citizen. I was abducted and brought here against my will. I will not answer your questions as your prisoner. If I am free, and if I have legal representation, or if I am in the presence of the police for a valid reason, I will answer your questions. Not before."

"We have ways to make you talk. So far we have been kind and patient with you. But you are forcing us to take other measures. We will find out what we wish to know. Your continued refusal to talk will bring harm to yourself and to your family. Do I make myself clear?"

"What has my family to do with this? They are old and know nothing. Why do you want to harm them?"

"We don't wish to harm them, but you will force us to, unless you cooperate."

Natasha didn't care what they did to her but the threat to harm her parents was cause for alarm. She now knew that she was dealing with the Mossad and also knew that they were ruthless and above the law. She had no one to call upon for help. She was alone in this matter and could survive only on her wits. She decided to create a scenario that might appease them so that they would not harm her parents and at the same time protect David, or at least buy him some time. She needed to get a message to him and could only do that if she were free.

"I would like a drink of water, please," she said.

"Are you ready to talk?"

"Give me a drink of water and I'll answer your first question as to how I became acquainted with David."

The man rose from his chair and left the room. He returned with a glass of water and held it to her mouth to drink.

"It would go much better if you untied my hands," she said.

"Drink. I'll consider that later."

Natasha drank until the glass was empty. Then she looked him in the eyes and said, "As you probably already know, David came to see me when I was assisting the Palestinians with their complaints against our government. He wanted to know why I was helping them. He told me that my actions might be considered the acts of a traitor against the state."

"And what was your reply?"

"I told him that I was performing an act of mercy."

"An act of mercy? Helping the Palestinians lodge a complaint against your country you consider an act of mercy?"

"I'm not going to justify my actions with you. I've answered your question. Now would you please let me go?"

"Did you have further contact with David after that?"

"If you expect me to answer any more of your questions, you will release me and take me home. I want to see that my parents are well."

"Do you have any knowledge of a training camp in Lebanon?"

"I will not answer any more of your questions until I am set free. I will answer your questions once I am in my own home without bondage."

The man left the room. She assumed he was conferring with his colleagues about their next move. She was skeptical that they would grant her wish yet she knew they wanted information and that she may be induced to cooperate on terms. She knew that they were in control and she could not readily escape. She needed time; time to get a message to David. She would give in just enough to gain some freedom of action.

***

Arnold decided to go the police station to see what he could learn about Richard Altman. He didn't know what to ask but he felt he needed to start somewhere. His efforts had produced no trace of a Richard Altman.

"If it's about a missing person, you need to fill out a missing person's report," said the officer.

"I'm not sure if the person is missing, it's just that I can find no trace of him. I thought perhaps you might help me," said Arnold.

"Why don't you tell me what you already know?"

Arnold told him about the original contact, the meeting at the Lions club, the dinner at his home, etc., and that there was no record anywhere of that name. He told him what he had already done in trying to locate a Richard Altman. "It's as though he and his wife just disappeared or never existed," said Arnold.

"Were you swindled in some way?"

"No, not in any monetary sense, but perhaps in another way. If I was given a false identity and misled, then I feel swindled. It makes me wonder why someone would do that. There must have been a reason."

"You say they claim to have come from Germany?"

"That's what they told me. And there is no record of any research firm connected with the university nor is there any record of a company doing medical research work that I could find, even with the Chamber of Commerce."

"I wouldn't be too concerned about it," said the officer. "I'll make a note of the name and bring it up at our morning meeting. If anyone hears anything connected with that name, I'll let you know. Since no crime has been committed, that's about all I can do."

Arnold thanked the officer and left the station. He would continue to ask questions and give a description. Surely someone will have seen or heard of them. He would also mention it at the next meeting of the Lion's club. The members would remember them. If they were seen, they would remember where and when.

***

Bernard Strauss hoped to see Brenda and James again. He enjoyed the conversation they had together and meeting them after the lecture was uncanny. Having reviewed in his mind the things they had discussed, he had some questions to ask since they seemed to be knowledgeable about events in the Middle East. He also found them to have a keen interest in the religious aspects concerning the people of the region. He waited for the promised phone call but it didn't come. He was frustrated with himself for not getting their phone number or address. He researched the telephone directory and called information. There was no listing for a James and Brenda Frey. He was perplexed. He returned to the café often on the chance that they may be there. He asked the manager, giving a description, but he couldn't remember seeing anyone like that. He said he would keep an eye out for them. Bernie left his address and phone number, just in case. So far, nothing. Remembering the work James had talked about, he checked on private medical research companies but there was no listing. He then checked with the university to see if they were engaged with a private medical research firm in the Ithaca area. There was none. Bernie was in a quandary. Did they lie to him? If so, why? Something wasn't kosher, he thought. They were here, and unless they left the area, they are still here. I will find them.

***

Jean and Caroline had accepted Samantha's explanation about their future status. It made sense. They obviously couldn't remain in the same area after completing the mission. It would be considered an act of terror and they could wind up on a wanted list. To get out of the country and then return with a clean slate was what they desired. Better still, perhaps their time would run out and they would have to leave before completing the mission. Trying to leave after the mission would be risky. They would both be questioned relentlessly. One wrong answer, and it would be all over. "Perhaps," said Jean, "we should make preparations to leave a few days before the time runs out. Yes, that's what we'll do. If we don't hear from Samantha with any further instructions, we'll leave together one week from today."

Caroline's eyes sparkled. She hoped for nothing more than to leave with Jean and not commit any crime. Now it was just a matter of time.

***

In South Carolina, Simone and Henry were becoming impatient. They wanted to get on with the mission and the unexplained delay was making them nervous. What was the hold up? Henry wondered. Has something gone wrong? He was anxious to talk with Samantha. They decided to wait a few more days and if she hadn't contacted them, they would use the emergency number to reach her. Time was running out and they would be forced to leave the country. They didn't want that. They wanted to complete the mission. And if they couldn't leave safely, then they would lose themselves in the vastness of America.

***

It was a long delay before someone entered the room where Natasha sat bound to the chair. Without any comment, the blindfold was reapplied and her arms and legs untied. She was taken by the arm and led out of the room. They walked down the same hallway, or so it seemed to Natasha, and then outside the building where she was placed in a car. The car ride felt like about the same length of time as when she was taken from her home. She made a mental estimate of the time it took and the number of turns the car had made that gave her a sense of direction. She realized that they may have taken a devious route, but it was still a piece of information she wanted to remember. When they pulled up to her house, the blindfold was removed and they accompanied her to the door. Natasha knocked at the door not wishing to startle her parents by walking in unannounced. There was no answer. She tried to open the door but it was locked. Natasha was surprised. They never locked their doors when they were home and that meant they were either not at home or didn't wish to be disturbed. She knocked again, waiting. She heard a movement inside and then a voice saying, "Who's there?"

"It's Natasha."

The door was opened a crack and then pulled wide open. Natasha recognized the face of their neighbor and without a greeting said, "Where is mother and father?"

"They went away but wouldn't say where they were going. They asked me to stay here in case you came back."

Natasha suspected they didn't leave voluntarily. Why would they not say where they were going? She said, "Did you see them go?"

"No, they called and asked me to look after the house and wait for you. They didn't say anything more. It sounded like they were in a hurry."

Natasha turned to the men standing by the door and said, "Where are my parents?"

"They're safe," said one of the men. "That's all you need to know." And to the neighbor he said, "You may go now."

The neighbor gave a curious glance at Natasha and noted the look of concern in her eyes. Natasha said nothing, and then nodded her head indicating that she should leave. The men gave her a menacing look as she made a hasty retreat. As soon as the neighbor was gone Natasha said, "What have you done with my parents?"

"We have complied with your request. You are in your home without bondage. Your neighbor confirmed to you that she talked to your parents and that they are okay."

"My neighbor didn't see them. How was she to know that they were okay?"

"You'll just have to take our word for that. Now we want some answers and you will answer them." He pulled out a chair for her to sit down at one side of the kitchen table. The men took a seat, one on each end of the table. Natasha didn't like this arrangement. They were too far away for her to reach them both at the same time. Now that her arms were free, if they were both next to her she would try to take them down. She wondered if the house had been searched. She was curious if the gun was still where she had hidden it. It would be a risk to go for it and then find it missing. Yet, what have I to lose? she thought. She was not concerned with her own safety but that of her parents and of course, David. She knew that he was somehow in trouble, or soon would be, and she needed to warn him. I need to stall and play along until an opportunity presents itself, she thought. There's always opportunity if one is ready and willing to take it. And if something happens to me, they will no longer have a reason to harm my parents or use them as leverage.

"What do you know about training camps in Lebanon," asked the smaller of the two men.

"I'm not sure I can answer your question. I understand, as does most everyone in our country, that there have been training camps in Lebanon," she said with sincerity.

"You know what I mean! I'm talking about recent training of men and women for a special mission. Now answer the question."

"And I repeat. I know that there are training camps in Lebanon. How am I supposed to know the purpose of the training?"

"Because we have reason to believe that you are connected with this training. What is David Levy's involvement in this?"

"You have just made an assumption and an accusation. You are trying to connect me with activity alleged to have taken place inside Lebanon, and you are trying to connect David Levy with that as well. I thought David was one of your people. Surely you know of his activities. Why would I have reason to be connected with David Levy or this training you speak of?"

"Be assured that we will find the answers. With your cooperation we can offer you immunity from any prosecution or retaliation. If you refuse to cooperate and give us the information we want, you will suffer the consequences, and they can be fatal. Are you denying that you have some connection with David Levy?"

"Of course I have had some connection with David Levy. I already told you that. I assume that he made a report about his contact with me."

"Are you saying that you only met him that one time?"

"No, I'm not saying that. I did see him again. He had some follow up questions and came to see me. Why don't you consult your own files and the reports he most surely had written? How else would you have connected me to David?"

They continued to press and Natasha persisted in thwarting them. Finally, with a bite in his voice, the taller of the two said, "We're leaving now but we're not finished with you. We have your parents and therefore advise you to remain near your home. If you try anything foolish you will be responsible for the consequences."

"What about my parents? When will I see them?"

The smaller man said, "When we are satisfied that you have no connection to David or the training in Lebanon. Until then, they will remain in our custody."

At that Natasha made a threat of her own. "If you harm my parents, I will find you and kill you."

They both rose from the table and left the house. Natasha waited until the car departed and then quickly left the house through the back door. She knew that fast action was required before a surveillance team was put in place. She needed to contact David and couldn't make that call from her house. She made her way to a friend's house making sure she wasn't followed. When she got there her friend was not at home but she knew where the key was kept and let herself in. She called the special coded number. She heard the strange sounds of cryptic devices until the connection was made. There was no answer. She left an urgent message that read: *"Suspect you of being part of training operation in Lebanon. Don't delay. Take care of yourself. I'll be OK."*

***

The next morning David got her message. He knew time was running out. He had to act fast. Once he disappeared from his office it would confirm their suspicions. The surveillance on him had tightened and his movements were becoming more restricted each day. It was no longer a question of "if" but rather "when" they would take him into custody. When that happened, it would be too late for everything. He had to act now.

David sent a message to his home office advising them that he would be out of town for a few days to follow up on some leads and that he would send a full report as soon as he returned. With that message sent, he packed a bag with the essentials he would need. The rest of his belongings he would abandon. He hoped that his message would serve to buy him a few days time before an all out search for him would begin. The first hurdle would be to leave without being followed. He made reservations for a room at the Sheraton hotel in the suburb, Newton, and then called a taxi. When the taxi arrived, he placed his bag in the taxi and told the driver to take it to the concierge at the Sheraton hotel in Newton. He paid the driver in advance with a handsome tip. David watched as the taxi drove away. He was sure that no car would follow the taxi; nevertheless he observed the tail talking into his cell phone. He may have made note of the cab number and would most likely inquire about the destination. Now he had to leave and lose him without creating suspicion. He left his office carrying his attaché and walked leisurely toward the subway. The tail followed. David knew he could lose them quickly, but that would alert them to his flight. He proceeded to the train station where the crowd of people at this hour of the day would help cover his movements. He purchased a newspaper and made his way to the lockers. Shielded by the crowd, he retrieved the small case and canvas bag with some articles of clothing he kept there. With his attaché case and newspaper he concealed the material and went directly into the men's room. He quickly changed his appearance using a wig, glasses and some make up. He took the jacket, necktie, and pair of slacks from the canvas bag and replaced them with the articles he was wearing. While he was making the alterations to his appearance, he kept looking through the crack in the door observing the people entering the men's room. He placed his attaché case and clothing he had removed into the canvas bag and left the men's room with just the one bag. He went straight to the subway, checking to see if he was being followed before entering. He felt relief that he had eluded the tail but knew that his disappearance would raise questions. Time was now his greatest enemy.

When David arrived at his Cambridge office, he called the Regent Hotel in Cambridge and made reservations under the name of John Miller. He then called the Sheraton hotel and talked to the reservations clerk. He cancelled the reservations that he had made for John Miller and then asked to speak to the concierge. The concierge confirmed that the luggage for a John Miller had arrived. David told the concierge that his plans had changed and asked him to kindly send John Miller's bag with a taxi to the Regent Hotel in Cambridge and to inform the taxi driver that the fee would be paid by the concierge on arrival. "You can confirm the cancellation at the reservations desk," said David. "If you wish, you can also confirm my new reservations at the Regent Hotel in Cambridge. Could you please take care of this at once? I will be waiting for my luggage."

The concierge said, "Consider it done, sir."

David walked the few blocks from his office to the hotel and talked with the concierge, telling him that he would be waiting in the coffee shop for the taxi with his luggage. He asked the concierge to notify him the moment it arrived so he could pay the driver. It was a half hour wait before the taxi arrived. David saw the concierge enter the coffee shop and went to meet him. He paid the cabbie and then gave a handsome tip to the concierge. He told the concierge that he hadn't checked in yet and had to leave on urgent business. He summoned another taxi and departed with his bag. He exited the cab two blocks from his office and walked the rest of the way. He then called the Regent Hotel and cancelled his reservation. Now he was free, at least for a short while, and he had the essential materials he needed to proceed with the mission.

The call he received from Natasha interfered with his plan to order the final amplification of the viruses. He placed a call to Albert, alias Richard Altman, and identified himself as Thomas

Miller. He gave the information concerning the quantities to be reproduced and wished to know how long that would take.

"I don't know Mr. Miller, but I will ask our employee Joyce. She is off today but I will ask her to come in tomorrow."

"I want you to call her today and have her come to your office as soon as possible. She must begin the work on the reproduction at once. I will call you again for a good estimate of the time required for her to finish the work."

"I will call her at once, sir," said Richard.

Richard called Joyce and let the phone ring until someone answered. The person on the phone said that Joyce was not in and that she was her roommate Carol. He left a message for Joyce to call a Mr. Altman as soon as she came in. Carol said she would give Joyce the message. She wrote a note for Joyce and left for her part-time waitress job.

Albert reflected on the call he had received from Mr. Miller and the sense of urgency in his voice. He knew the mission was now in the final stage and it caused him to think about the action they were soon to take. Instead of feeling elated as he had originally anticipated, there was a feeling of some reluctance. What has come over me? he thought. Why do I feel this way? Surely I knew it would eventually happen. He tried to shake the feeling but it wouldn't go away. He decided to discuss it with Mary when he got home. He wondered how she would feel when he confided to her the order he had received to reproduce the viruses. He was pacing back and forth when the phone rang.

"Altman here," said Richard.

"Mr. Altman. This is Joyce. I just got your message."

"I need to speak with you at once. I have something important to discuss with you."

"Can you tell me what this is all about?"

"I will give you the detail's when you get here."

"I'm sorry Mr. Altman, but I already have plans for the evening."

"Break your plans if you must, but it is important that I see you."

"I will try, Mr. Altman but it won't be easy."

"I understand that, but it is important. I will wait for you."

***

Carol didn't necessarily like working as a waitress but needed the extra money. She felt fortunate to be working at a restaurant that catered to others besides the college crowd. Tonight it was extra busy and she expected greater tips from the adults at the table she was serving. As she was placing food on the table she heard the name Altman mentioned. She found that curious since she had just written that name down in a message for Joyce. The man sitting at the head of the table was talking and she heard him say, "I have been trying to locate this Richard Altman and he seems to have disappeared or is non-existent."

"Did you contact the police," asked his friend.

"I have contacted the police, the university and even the Chamber of commerce, but there is no one with that name associated with them to be found in this area."

"Excuse me," Carol said. I couldn't help hearing you mention the name, Altman. I don't know if it is the same person, but I took a message for my roommate this evening from a Mr. Altman."

"A Richard Altman?" said the man.

"I didn't get a first name. I was asked to have my roommate call a Mr. Altman and he gave me the number to call."

"Do you have the number?"

"No. I wrote it down but I don't remember the number. I'm sure my roommate will have it though."

"Good. May I ask you to get the number and call me? Here's my card. I'd really appreciate it. It may not be the person I'm looking for, but then again it could be."

"Of course," said Carol. She took the card and read the name Arnold Myers. She placed the card in her pocket and continued with her work. She found it curious with the coincidence of the name and wondered why the man was looking for this Mr. Altman. She decided to get the number from Joyce when she got home.

***

Joyce arrived at the office and Richard immediately asked her to take a seat by his desk. "I'm sorry to call you on such a short notice, but I received a call from our parent company and they asked for immediate action. I trust you understand," he said.

"I understand how business works and that there are always emergencies of some sort," she said.

He handed her a sheet of paper with the amount of virus desired for the two categories. She was not privy to the distinction concerning the virus designation for fish and the other for birds. "Based on the quantities indicated, I need to know how long it will take you to make these amplifications and I need that information tonight. I'll let you alone so you can do the calculation."

(The amplification process would normally take weeks to complete. Acceleration was possible due to the advanced techniques developed by the foreign scientists they applied to the strains of virus being used.)

It did not take her long to make the calculations, yet there were some stipulations concerning certain supplies that would be required in order to complete the task. Richard looked at the list and knew he could get them within a day's time with a special order and overnight service.

"If I understand this correctly, it will take you three days to complete the reproductions once you have all the material. Is that correct?"

"Yes, that is working full time, and provided I receive the required substances from your other lab. Of course my studies..."

"Until this is completed, you will have to forget about your studies. You need to devote full time to this. And I want to remind you about the confidentiality of what you are doing. Nothing, absolutely nothing about the work and anyone involved with this project can be discussed. I will let you know when you will be free to discuss your work. Is that clear?"

"Yes, sir. Very clear."

"You can start the work at once. Let me know the substances required and I will arrange it."

"I will be here first thing in the morning," said Joyce, and she left the office.

Richard waited for Mr. Miller's call. In the meanwhile he placed an order for the materials Joyce needed. As he expected, he could get the materials the following day with overnight service. Richard was pleased to have the information requested of him.

When David got off the phone with Albert, he called Samantha. She was excited to get his call and to know that he was okay. He briefly explained what had happened and that the mission was now in full motion, waiting only for the required amount of virus to be ready for distribution.

"I'm moving to a new location tomorrow and want you to join me," said David. Fly into Philadelphia, and as soon as you land, call me on my cell phone. I'll let you know where to go from there."

The conversation ended and Samantha made immediate travel arrangements. Just the thought of being with David made her heart race. She decided not to call Caroline and Jean and let them leave the country without any further contact. Any discussion with them would only cause questions that she did not wish to answer. She placed a call to Simone and Henry saying that things were now in an action mode and that they would hear from her very shortly. Henry was pleased to hear that and said, "We are ready." Since David had been in contact with Albert, she erroneously assumed that Albert would inform James and Brenda.

***

It was late when Carol got back to her dorm. She was pleased with the amount of tips she received, but was tired. Joyce was already in bed and she decided not to disturb her. She would wait until morning to ask her about Mr. Altman. She looked for the note she had left for Joyce. It wasn't there.

Joyce heard Carol come in, but remained quiet. She wanted to get up early and be fresh to start the project. She lay in bed wondering why there was suddenly such a rush. She wanted to complete the task within the time frame she had given Richard; she would not compromise safety for speed. And the secrecy involved was a bit unnerving. She wondered about the use of the viruses. And the quantities they were requesting made no sense. If it was for further research why did they require such quantities? Oh well, she thought, I am getting paid to do a job and not to ask questions.

***

Joyce had a troubled sleep and her alarm clock woke her with a start. She looked at the clock and knew if she hurried she would have time for some cereal and a cup of coffee before leaving. She hoped that the alarm had not awakened Carol. She got dressed and was putting on the coffee when Carol said, "You are up bright and early this morning."

"Yes, I just have time for a quick bite and some coffee and then I'm off to work."

"Did you get my message that I left?"

"Yes, thanks Carol. I appreciate it."

"Who is Mr. Altman?"

"He's my boss where I'm working. He called to ask me to come in to work."

"What kind of work do you do? I mean, we never really talked about it. And what kind of a person is this Mr. Altman?"

"Why are you asking me these questions all of a sudden? Besides, my work is confidential. I'm sorry, but I'm not at liberty to discuss it."

"Hmmm. This sure is interesting. Last night I overheard a conversation where someone was trying to locate a Richard Altman. I remembered the name from taking the phone call but there was no first name. Would this Mr. Altman's first name be Richard?"

"Yes, it is. But why do you need to know that?"

"I spoke to the man who had mentioned Mr. Altman's name and told him that I had taken a call from a Mr. Altman."

"What? You told a stranger about a personal call?"

"Yes, I did. What's the matter with that?"

"I don't know if there is anything the matter, but why would you give out information about a person contacting me to a total stranger? I think that is wrong."

"The man is just trying to locate him. He asked me if I could give him the telephone number and I said I would."

"No! You can't do that!" I will not permit it!" She took a last sip of her coffee, grabbed her coat and purse and left, slamming the door behind her.

Carol sat on the edge of her bed bewildered. What has come over Joyce? Why wouldn't she give me the man's number? There is something not right here. That is not like Joyce. I've got to find out what she's doing. I did promise the gentlemen that I'd get the number for him.

She realized that he gave her his card but hadn't even asked for her name or phone number. Well, at least he can't call me about it, she thought. She turned over and went back to sleep.

CHAPTER 17
PURSUIT

The Chief put down the report, removed his glasses, and rubbed his eyes. He replaced his glasses and once again looked at the report and asked, "When was the last time David was seen."

"He was seen last on the date he sent his message," said his adjutant. "Our surveillance team was not aware of the message he sent to us. When he didn't return to his apartment that night, they reported that fact."

"Two men watching, and he evaded both of them?"

"Yes. They became suspicious when he placed a bag in a cab without getting in himself. They got the number of the cab and learned that the destination was to the Sheraton hotel in Newton. That's a suburb outside of Boston. When they got there it was too late. There were no reservations under David's name. Naturally he would have used a bogus name. From the concierge they learned that a Mr. Miller called, said that his reservation was cancelled and asked that the bag be sent to the Regent hotel in Cambridge, and to send it by cab. By the time our men got there the bag had already been retrieved and the trace ended there. The description of the man who picked up the bag was not that of David. Either he used a disguise or he had someone else get the bag for him."

"Why is David on the run? That's what we must find out. Was anything found in his office that would give us a clue to where he might have gone?" said the chief.

"Nothing sir. It was clean."

"Get out a message to our regional offices that David is missing. Perhaps he contacted someone. In any event, have them be on the lookout for him. I find it most curious that David disappears after you talked to this Natasha person. I suspect a connection between them and the training in Lebanon. Keep digging. We need answers." The chief drummed his fingers on the desk. "Have you talked to that Palestinian girl that David got so worked up about when our boys were questioning her? I believe her name was Samantha."

"No, sir, we haven't."

"Find her and see what she knows. Anybody known to have been associated with David that was in any way connected to the Palestinians should be questioned."

"Perhaps we made a mistake in allowing Natasha to go home, sir, but we weren't getting anywhere with our questions. She's too clever – too well trained. The only leverage we have with her is her parents. If we lose that card we'll get nothing more from her."

The chief slammed down the report on his desk. "Use it. We got to find out who is planning what, where, and when. These terrorists must be stopped."

***

After Natasha left her message for David, she returned home without being observed. She removed the covering tile on the side of the bathtub. This particular tile was used to cover the access to the plumbing under the tub. She reached in and was relieved to feel the plastic sack. She pulled it out, opened the sack, and removed the gun. She opened and closed the loaded chamber noting that it was still well lubricated and would function without a problem. The box of extra cartridges she had placed in a separate plastic sack was also there. Holding the gun in her hand gave her more confidence. She would not hesitate to use it if it became necessary, and she believed that it would. She knew that the

Mossad would not give up until they were satisfied they had the answers they sought. And they would use any means to get it.

She feared for her parents. She knew that they would be defiant with their captors and would want her to take whatever steps she felt she needed without worrying about their safety. Just the thought of that made her proud of them. They had felt the same sympathy for the Palestinians and the indignation about their treatment as she had. They had often expressed their regret in leaving the land of their birth. They just didn't fit into the Israeli society and longed for the open spaces of their homeland. The decision to immigrate had been for her sake, thinking that she would have better opportunities in Israel. They shared her disappointment.

As she sat thinking these things, there was a knock on the door. She quickly closed the tile but kept the pistol. There was no time to conceal it on her person so she carried it with her and placed it on the shelf behind the door where it was not visible. She asked, "Who's there."

"Open the door. We have a few questions."

She didn't recognize the voice but knew it was the Mossad. To refuse to open only meant they would force the door open. She opened it and stood within reach of the shelf. They entered and closed the door behind them. Both men were new to her. Another tag team, she assumed. She didn't invite them to sit down nor did she move from her position. "What do you want?" she asked.

"What do you know about a girl named Samantha?" said the taller of the two.

Natasha was surprised at the question but maintained her nondescript expression. "Samantha?"

"Yes, Samantha Anabtawi. We have reason to believe that you know this girl."

Natasha believed that they already did know. She had become acquainted with Samantha through David and they had been seen together. To deny any knowledge of Samantha would only aggravate the situation. She said, "Yes, I knew a Samantha, but I don't know where she is, if that's what you want to know."

"You can make it easier on yourself if you cooperate, and I believe you know what I mean by that. Tell us what you know about Samantha and her connection with David Levy."

"I believe you already know about her connection to David Levy. He saved her from your torture. Everyone in Palestine knows about that incident. Of course that would be kept secret from our own citizens," she said in contempt.

"Were you with Samantha in Lebanon?" the small one asked, being careful to watch her reaction.

"What would I be doing in Lebanon? If you want to know if Samantha was in Lebanon, you'll have to ask her."

"You're still trying to be coy with us. You're digging a deeper hole for yourself and one that you won't be able to climb out of. You know we will find the answers to these questions. Now why don't you just tell us the truth? It will save us all a lot of time and you a lot of pain."

"You're threatening me again?"

"No, we're taking you in and this time you may not be coming out." The smaller man reached for her arm as the taller one moved to her side. She reacted instantly giving a karate kick that knocked the man in front of her to the floor. With her elbow she hit the man at her side in the stomach. When he doubled over she brought up her knee and caught him under the chin knocking him out. The man on the floor was struggling to his feet. A swift kick to the side of his head knocked him out. Natasha grabbed the gun on the shelf and went into the bathroom to get the extra shell cartridges. She picked up the small case she had packed and went out the back door. She made her way along a path she had used often when she needed to get away quickly without being observed. She knew there was no coming back. She needed to get into the Palestinian territory where she could be hidden. Her situation was desperate and she would not hesitate to use her weapon if anyone tried to stop her. If they took her into custody she would not come out alive.

***

Samantha arrived in Philadelphia carrying a gift package. She wanted to give David something special and couldn't think of what he may like until she saw the red feather sticking out of the Bavarian hat. She pictured David in the Alps with a hiking stick wearing that hat. She was pleased with the picture that formed in her mind; and so on impulse she purchased the hat. As soon as she exited the plane in Philadelphia she placed the call to David's cell phone and he answered immediately.

"I just arrived," she said.

"Good. Take a taxi to the Residence Inn. It's about a half mile from the airport. Come to room number eight."

"Okay. See you soon," she said, and disconnected the call. The smile on her face reflected how she felt. She walked directly to the taxi stand and gave the order for the Residence Inn. She had packed the few things she needed in a carry-on bag and avoided baggage claim. She saw the signs indicating the Residence Inn's own transport service but the use of a taxi avoided contact with others who may be guests at the Inn. That was certainly in David's mind when he told her to take a taxi.

David stood by the window waiting for her. He could feel his heart race when he saw her alight from the taxi. She carried a single bag and a box under her arm. He wore no disguise and waited for her to come straight to the room. Before she could knock he opened the door and she came in flushed with excitement, dropped her bag, and went into his arms. David used his foot to close the door and they stood where they were hugging each other. Then they kissed and their passion surfaced at once. No words were spoken as he removed her jacket and led her to the bedroom.

***

Inquiry at Beirut's airport took some time. With some bribes the undercover agents were able to gather some sketchy information from passport control, security, and passenger records for airlines flying to the west. They learned that eight young people, both men and women, had departed Beirut with student visas. Four had departed for Germany and four had departed for France. In Germany they learned that four persons of Lebanese origin were in violation for their length of stay. In France they also learned that four persons of Lebanese origin were in violation. The agent's reports to their headquarters in Tel-Aviv served to confirm suspicions about suspected persons from the training camp in Lebanon departing for the west.

The agency chief read the reports. If there were Palestinians involved and possibly Israeli citizens, then the passports had to be forgeries, but where did they get them? An inquiry was made to the Israeli passport office but there was nothing unusual about any passports issued to Israeli citizens. The list they reviewed did not meet the profiles they sought. The chief asked his adjutant to check with known forgers used by the agency. Their agents often required false identity papers as part of their work. "It has to be one of the forgers who created the false passports," he said. "Check with all of them and find out what work they have done recently and who ordered it. Specifically I want to know what forger David Levy may have used. Check on that first."

***

A few days later, the special agent assigned to check on forgers took a seat in the chief's office. The file he carried with him he placed in front of the chief saying, "It's all there sir. It took some pressure, but I was able to get the information."

The chief read the report and then said, "If I understand this correctly, the man prepared seven Israeli passports and five German passports, but there were no names attached to them. And they were ordered by David Levy?"

"Yes, sir. I think David was being very cautious in not having one person do the entire job. He obviously has another person affixing the names and photos."

"Who might have placed names in the passports?"

"I don't know that sir. Whoever he was, he was not one of our known forgers."

"It does confirm that David is involved in some clandestine operation. And it seems to tie into the training activity in Lebanon. We need to find David and also to notify Interpol about false identities. I'll handle that. You've done a good job. If you can find anything further, let me know at once."

"Thank you, sir," said the agent, feeling pleased with himself. He knew David and they had been friends. It was uncommon to become close friends with anyone in the agency but he knew David to be a serious operative, an honest and sensitive person. Perhaps too sensitive for his own good, he thought. That got him into trouble when he interfered with the interrogation of the Palestinian. One cannot be in this business and have high moral values and survive. He remembered what was told to him by his supervisor during his first year with the agency. He said that those who survive in this business do so by following orders without question. And that's what he had tried to do. Secretly, he hoped that David would not be found. "He must have a good reason for his actions," he said to himself as he left the building.

***

Israeli security was informed concerning their suspicions and they in turn informed Homeland Security in the USA. They were told that there were terrorist suspects, possibly carrying Israeli and German passports, that may have traveled to America or were in the process of traveling there. And it may have occurred within the past 45 - 90 days.

When Homeland Security received the information, they sent a message to the immigration and passport control departments of all international airports to be on the lookout for young men or women between the ages of 18 and 35 arriving with Israeli or German passports. They were ordered to hold these people for questioning. A separate request was made to check records for arrivals within the past three months for people carrying Israeli passports with visas. Homeland Security was to be notified immediately if any such records were found.

***

The assault on the Agents and subsequent disappearance of Natasha was reported immediately to the chief. He was angry that a woman could take out two of his people and disappear so easily.

An immediate search of the area turned up nothing. Natasha's actions proved that she had something to hide and they were bent on finding her. Based on the skills she had demonstrated, they believed that she had been one of the women trainers in Lebanon. They had her parents, but it did them little good to be holding them unless she could be found. They believed that Natasha would try to contact her parents if she knew where they were being held. A few days later, after planting bugs in the house, they took her parents home and placed a 24-hour watch on their house. It was a simple three-room apartment with a front and back door that consisted of a small kitchen, a bedroom, living room and a small bath. No one could enter or leave without being noticed.

Natasha's escape without detection was not a surprise to anyone in the agency or to herself. She was an expert in evasive tactics, and once she had entered the West Bank, she felt more secure. From there she could enter Jordan or Syria with the aid of friends should that become necessary. She thought of her parents and knew that her escape rendered their captivity useless. She would find out what she could concerning their welfare should they be released. She wondered about the mission and hoped it would succeed. All the people associated with the training had strong reasons for revenge and the teams were in position to carry it out. But what of David? Was he okay? Was he in a position to carry out the mission? She would try to let him know that she was safe and give a further warning. She was sure that she, along with the rest of the world, would hear about the mission once it was carried out.

***

The materials Richard had ordered were delivered as promised, but he was troubled. Joyce told him about her roommate's questions and that people had been asking about him. She said that she thought he should know. He asked her to tell him exactly what was discussed and she had tried to tell him word for word. She wanted him to understand that she was maintaining the confidentiality that she had promised. Joyce was working tirelessly and would complete the job on schedule if nothing happened to interfere. Richard was now waiting to hear from Mr. Miller or Samantha so he could give them his report and wait for further instructions. He had talked to James the previous day. James had seemed a bit nervous realizing that they would soon be engaged in the final act of the mission.

***

When James got home he told Brenda about the impending event and she too became nervous. "What is happening to us?" she said. "Why do I feel this way?"

"I know what you mean," he said. "Now that it is almost time to carry it out I'm wondering if it is the right thing to do. I mean if there was more time and more Americans became aware of what is happening to our people, perhaps things would change."

"I feel the same way. But they did kill our parents and we promised ourselves that we would take revenge. Was it wrong for us to feel that way?"

"No, I don't think it was wrong. It was natural to feel that way. And we chose to join up to take out our revenge on the country that is supporting acts of terror."

"Did you say acts of terror?"

"Yes, I did, didn't I? We keep hearing about Muslim terrorists and that hits us personally. Why don't we hear about Israeli terrorists or American terrorists? In reality those who support those terrorists are themselves terrorists. I think that President Bush tried to make a point about that by saying that those who harbor terrorists would themselves be considered terrorists and he particularly tied that statement to Syria. I suppose with that logic, Bush is a terrorist and America a terrorist country."

"This is all so complicated and ridiculous, don't you think?"

"Yes, I agree. But we can't back out now, can we?" he said with earnest.

"I don't know. It would be bad for us to back out. We would be letting the others down. Yet deep down I don't want to do it. I keep thinking about all the people who will die - innocent people. I keep thinking about Bernie. He's such a nice man. By doing this we won't be any better than those who killed our people."

He thought about what she said and nodded his head in agreement. Then with sudden realization he said, "Do you realize that we have just a few days before we must leave here? We must return to Canada in order to catch our flight back to Frankfurt; otherwise we'll be in trouble with the authorities and have much explaining to do. If we ever intend to return here, we can't let our visas expire without an extension request."

"Do you suppose if there is no order to proceed within the next two days that we could inquire about returning?"

"That's a thought. I'll ask Albert about it. He is the one in contact with Samantha."

***

Carol noted that Joyce had been coming home very late at night for the past two days and her curiosity got the best of her. All this secrecy about a job didn't make sense. She decided to follow Joyce and see where she went each day. She took special care not to be noticed. She put on a hat large enough to tuck her hair into it, wore dark glasses, and carried a large shopping bag that could be used to shield her face. They boarded a campus bus and Joyce never even looked in her direction. They both got off the bus at the end of the campus. Carol walked behind the bus waiting for it to pull out. She then saw that Joyce was taking the path through the park. Carol followed at a safe distance and watched as Joyce entered an office-building complex. She waited until Joyce was in the building and then followed her inside. There was no one there – not even a receptionist. Joyce had gone into some office, but which one? Most of the doors showed the name of a firm and some just had the name of a person. She kept looking for a Richard Altman but there was no such name on any of the doors. The office directory at the front didn't show that name either. She tried to find a name that might sound like a medical research firm, but there was no such name listed. Carol finally gave up and left. She made a note of the address of the building. At least I can give Mr. Myers an address, she thought. It will be up to him to find Mr. Altman.

Carol placed the call and it was answered with, "Arnold Myers here."

"Hi, this is Carol. I don't know if you remember me, but you gave me your card at the Applebee's restaurant last week. I was the waitress serving your table. You were looking for a Mr. Altman, I believe."

"Yes, of course I remember. I forgot to get your name and number and I'm glad you called. Do you have the number?"

"No, not the number, but I think I might have an address. My roommate would not give me a number, but I know where she works. I don't know if that will help you but it is all that I have."

"That's fine, Carol. What's the address?"

She gave him the address describing the building and Arnold thanked her for her efforts. He said he would let her know if he had any success in locating Richard Altman.

Arnold had the afternoon free and decided to drive by the office and see if he could find his friend Richard. Surely there was some explanation to all of this. He realized, to his chagrin, that he had failed again to get Carol's telephone number. Perhaps the same thing had happened in not having Richard's phone number. He felt foolish for being so careless. Perhaps old age was creeping up on him. He realized that he should have used his cell phone. That would have recorded the number. But he still refused to carry it everywhere he went and used it only for emergencies. He was not about to walk around like many with their hand seemingly pasted to their ears and be interrupted with a phone ringing at the most inopportune times. He hated it when someone's cell phone rang disturbing others around them. No, he wasn't ready to be a party to that, at least not yet.

Arnold entered the building and looked at the directory. There was no research firm listed. He checked for a consulting firm and there was no name with that word in the name. Of course not all consulting or research firms have the designation of what they do in the name of the firm. He therefore tried using the process of elimination. There were twelve company names shown on the directory and two spaces left blank. Arnold assumed that the blank ones were not occupied. He dismissed the obvious ones - the franchised employment agency, accounting firm, insurance agency and a local real estate company. The remainders were unknown to him. He decided to enter the other offices and inquire if there was a Richard Altman there. He got a "no" at each office and the only two doors remaining were blank. He tried the knob of the first door and it was locked. He tried the second one and it opened, so he walked in. Someone was obviously using this space since it was furnished. He said, "Hello. Is anyone here?" There was no answer so he walked further into the office and again said, "Hello, hello."

Joyce was working in the lab with the door closed but heard someone calling hello. She wondered why Richard hadn't answered. Perhaps he had stepped out but he certainly wouldn't leave the door unlocked. She carefully placed the bottle she was handling in the holder, removed her gloves, and went out to see who it was. Just as she got to the door it opened. A man was standing there with a puzzled expression. Joyce was alarmed to see a stranger in the office, especially when he was about to enter the lab. She quickly closed the door behind her and stepped out. "What are you doing here?" she said.

"I'm sorry to disturb you and hope I haven't startled you. I'm looking for a Mr. Altman and heard that he may work in this building. I tried the door; it was unlocked so I just walked in."

Joyce didn't know what to say. It was curious that there was no name of the company on the registry and nothing on the office door. Richard only talked about the confidentiality of their work. How was she to answer this person? Carol had also wanted to know about Richard. What is going on? she thought. What's this person doing here?

"I'm sorry Mr...."

"My name is Arnold Myers. I met a Richard Altman at our Lions Club. We also had dinner together but I failed to get his phone number and since that time I have been unable to locate him. I heard that a Mr. Altman might work in this building so I came here in the chance that I might find him. I don't even know if it is a Richard Altman that may work here. I suppose I have struck out again, eh?"

"Mr. Myers. I don't know what to tell you. If you will leave your card when my boss returns I will give it to him. Perhaps he may know the person you are looking for."

"That's fine. I'd appreciate it. What do you do here if I may ask?"

"I'm sorry but I'm not at liberty to discuss my work. I will give your card to my boss, Mr. Myers."

She led him to the door and opened it. She said goodbye and when he had stepped outside, she locked the door. Arnold heard the door being locked. He stood there for a few moments trying to understand what had just happened. Now his curiosity was peaked. What are they doing in there? And I blew it again. I didn't ask the young lady for her name. She may have been the roommate of Carol.

He decided he would call Carol and get a description of her roommate. If there were a match, then he would decide what to do.

If Arnold had waited another five minutes, he would have met Richard returning to the office. Richard unlocked the door and went to his desk. When Joyce heard the door open, she came out to see who it was. "Mr. Altman," she said. "I'm glad you're back."

"Is there a problem?"

"A man came in a short time ago. He just walked in. He said the door was unlocked. He was looking for a Richard Altman."

Richard's face turned red. He realized that he must have forgotten to lock the door. "Who was it?"

Joyce handed the card to Richard. "The man gave me this card. He said that he heard a Mr. Altman worked in this building and was trying to locate him. He said he had met Richard Altman at a Lions club and later had dinner with him but forgot to get his phone number. He didn't know if the Mr. Altman that worked in this building was the same Richard Altman. Since you were not here, I didn't tell him that it was you."

Richard felt relieved and yet alarmed. "Thanks Joyce," he said. "You did the right thing. We have tried to keep our work confidential and that includes those working here." To change the subject he said, "How are you coming with your work?"

"I expect to complete it by tomorrow evening, as long as there are no more interruptions."

"Good. I will see that you have a nice bonus in your pay for getting it done on time."

Joyce was pleased to hear that and went back to work. She couldn't erase what had transpired but determined to push it out of her mind. She had a job to do and that's what she would concentrate on. The bonus sounded wonderful.

Richard sat at his desk with his hands propped under his chin. How could I have been so careless? he thought. At least I wasn't here when he came. It would have been difficult to answer his questions. Should I call him or try to avoid him? That was a question he couldn't answer. Everything was coming to a head and outside interference was something he needed to avoid. He wondered if he should mention it to Samantha or to Mr. Miller. He determined to discuss it with Mary when he got home.

CHAPTER 18
LAUNCH ORDER

Night turned into day. David and Samantha savored every moment together and didn't want it to end. It was almost noon when David forced himself to get up and attend to business. He asked Samantha to contact Albert and see if the virus preparations were ready. If so, he gave her the instructions that she was to give Albert.

Samantha placed the call to Albert with David listening in. Albert answered the phone, "Altman here."

"Hi Richard, this is Rover. Is the project completed?"

"It is expected to be finished tomorrow."

"Excellent. As soon as you can, take 1/3 of the product and prepare it for shipment to Team #3. You have the packing and handling instructions. Call HL (Henry Lerew) and let him know when to expect the package. Ask him to call you back for further instructions when it arrives."

Samantha gave him Henry's phone number in the numeric code they had previously devised. Then she said, "Inform Team #2 that they should be ready within the next few days to begin. I'll call you back tomorrow to confirm that everything is ready."

While Richard was on the phone, James entered the office. This was unusual since he was to avoid coming into the office while Joyce was working. Richard realized that there had been no opportunity for James to come to the office ever since Joyce began the final phase of her work, and that lasted late into the evening. Richard motioned for him to come into his office and close the door, just as he hung up the phone.

"I'm surprised to see you," said Richard. "I wanted to see you anyway and was going to call you, but we can talk now."

"You wanted to see me?" said James.

"Yes, but you must have had a reason to come here. "What's up?"

James appeared nervous. He rubbed his hands together, and then stroked his jaw before replying. "We have been through a lot together, haven't we?"

"Yes, we have, and we've come a long way since then. Something's troubling you. What's on your mind?"

"Brenda and I have had much discussion in the past week or so. It began after the forum that we attended at the university. I told you about that."

"Yes, you did."

"Well, we also met some people and had interesting discussions about our part of the world. With what we heard and the people we met, we became troubled about what we are in the process of doing. Last night we reached a decision and wanted to discuss it with you. I came alone but I also speak for Brenda."

Richard was reluctant to ask him for the decision they had reached because he thought he knew what it was, but there was no avoiding it. "Tell me about it," he said.

"The short answer is that we don't want to carry out our part of the mission and would like to return home before our visas expire. We realize that we made a commitment to do it, and wanted to do it, but we don't feel the same way anymore. We want you to know how much we regret this decision and realize what a bind that may put you in, but that's how we feel."

Richard tried not to show any emotion. He could understand. He and Mary had tried to avoid further discussion about the mission but the impending event was wearing on both of them as well. He secretly wished that it was he sitting in the chair talking instead of the one listening. Now it was Richard's turn to rub his chin while he decided how to respond. Before he could say anything, James said, "You said that you wanted to see me. What was that about?"

"Samantha asked me to talk to you. I was on the phone with her when you came in. I was asked to inform you that you should be ready to commence within the next few days."

James bowed his head. He realized the position it would put Albert in. Albert was his friend; they had both suffered the same fate in Iraq. They had trained together and were the first chosen for the mission. Now he was telling his friend that he was backing out. He looked up and directly into Albert's eyes but he didn't see Albert, he saw Ahmed. At that same moment as they stared at one another Albert saw Yussef. He saw them shaking hands over a table in that small café in Beirut. He remembered the elation they felt to be embarking on a mission to avenge their families and start a new life. Now here they sat across the desk from one another, in another world, contemplating an entirely different decision. Was it going to end this way? Could he and Mary carry out the mission alone? What would Samantha say?

"James, since you have already thought things through and have taken the decision not to go through with it, there's nothing I wish to say to change your mind. You are my friend and I will try to protect you as best I can. I suggest that you leave at once. Do it today. I would rather tell the boss you have already gone than to say that you are contemplating it."

"Do you mean it? Won't this put you in a bind?"

"Yes, I mean it. I would love to say goodbye to Brenda as well but there's no time. I expect the order to come as early as tomorrow to proceed with the mission. It will make things easier to tell them that you have already gone than try and explain that you are still here but don't want to go through with it."

"Thanks Albert. I hope to see you again. I appreciate your understanding. I think you know that Brenda and I will be married as soon as we can. I only wish you were there to stand with us."

"Go, and God be with you, my friend," said Albert." He reached into his desk drawer and took out a handful of currency that he handed to James. This will help you get back. I wish there was more to give you but I didn't know it would be needed so soon.

"Thanks," said James. They shook hands, and then embraced. James turned and left the office without looking back.

***

When Jean and Caroline had not heard anything from Samantha in the several days following their dinner together, they had taken that silence as permission to leave. They had spent a few days doing the things they had come to enjoy, and then had set the date to depart. Once their reservations were confirmed, Jean had cancelled all personal services to be effective the date of departure. He had deposited the key to the apartment in the mailbox of the landlord, returned the leased car and had taken a taxi to the airport. They were now at the airport in Atlanta getting ready to board the aircraft. The attendant at the check-in counter looked at their passports and visas. Noting the Israeli passports, they were flagged. The notice from Homeland Security had been distributed to all airline personnel in a meeting and then posted at each check-in counter. Check in personnel were to notify security if anyone with an Israeli passport between the ages of 18 and 35 checked in. While they were waiting in the departure lounge they heard their names being paged to come to the desk. They approached the desk smiling without concern for the two men in uniform standing alongside.

"Caroline Bardot and Jean Dupont?" said the attendant.

"Yes, that's us," said Jean with a wide grin.

The two men standing alongside the desk approached and said, "May I see your passports please?"

They were handed to the man who looked at them and then said, "Please come with us"

"What's the problem," asked Jean. "Is something not in order?"

"We have a few questions – just a formality."

They were led outside the departure lounge and along the corridor to a side office. Jean knew that something was wrong and wondered if it had something to do with their length of stay. They were five days ahead of the expiration date shown on their visas, so that couldn't be the problem. He decided to wait and see. He reviewed in his mind the training they had received if questioned by the authorities. They were taught that most of the time it was a 'fishing' expedition and that remaining calm was their first and foremost defense. They knew that they were traveling with false identities and that the passports were forgeries, but that had not concerned them. When they arrived in the States without any questions about their documents, they had felt safe. And since they had not committed any illegal act while here, Jean wasn't too concerned.

They were seated in front of an immigrations officer. He did not rise to greet them. He looked at the passports and then said, "What was the purpose of your visit to America?"

Jean said pleasantly, "My friend and I wanted to spend a holiday in America and see if we were meant for each other. He looked at Caroline and took her hand. We have decided to get married, and now we're on our way home. Once we're married we want to return to America. We have fallen in love with your country."

It took the immigrations officer by surprise. He couldn't help but smile and offer his congratulations. According to the papers in front of him, everything appeared to be in order and he saw no need to detain to detain them. Then he asked, "Where is your home."

Carrying an Israeli passport and traveling east could only suggest that they would be returning to Israel. Jean paused for a moment and then said, "Most recently we have been living in France, but for the ceremony we will be traveling to Israel."

The immigrations officer noted the hesitation. He felt it would be better if someone were there who spoke Hebrew and could ask a few questions. He was a veteran and was not a person to be hurried just because the final call for the flight had been made. If they missed the flight they could catch another one. He felt more questions were needed and as well as confirmation of the language. He picked up the phone and called his office.

"I need someone at the departure lounge who can speak Hebrew. Is anyone available?"

"Not at the moment," said the Sergeant, "but Hal Wallach will be here in about an hour. Do you want me to send him down when he arrives?"

The immigrations officer was looking at both passengers while talking on the phone and noticed how uncomfortable Miss Bardot became. The glance she gave Jean Dupont showed concern, perhaps even alarm. He decided to hold them until Hal Wallach arrived. If everything was okay, they could catch another flight. He was nearing retirement and wanted his record to show that he was thorough in his job. He said, "Yes, send him down to my office as soon as he comes in."

He called the departure lounge and told them not to hold the flight. He knew their bags were already on board and to retrieve them would require unnecessary delay of the flight. There was no security risk in this instance since their bags had already been screened and would have been accompanied by the passengers.

The officer then said, "I'm sorry to delay you in this manner, and I'm afraid you will miss your flight. A colleague of mine will have a few questions to ask you. He will be along within the hour. Once you are cleared, we will assist you with another flight."

Jean was perspiring. He didn't look at Caroline and tried his best to remain calm when he said, "I don't understand. Our papers are in order. Our visas have not expired. Why are we being detained?"

"As I mentioned to you before, it's a formality. Security has been tightened due to a terrorist threat and we're following instructions. I'm sure you understand. I know it's an inconvenience but it is for the safety of all of us. May we offer you refreshment? Coffee, tea or a soda?"

Jean's throat was dry and he needed something to drink. He was sure Caroline felt the same way and said, "Yes, please. Water would be fine. You also Caroline?"

"Yes. Please."

The officer sent his assistant for the water and then excused himself saying, "I'll be back shortly. Just relax. There are magazines on the table. If there's anything else you need, just ask Mr. Jones."

They sat alone and stared at each other. Jean didn't want to say anything since the office might be set up for eavesdropping. Hidden cameras may also be in place. He tried to sound calm when he said, "This is sure an inconvenience, but these things do happen. We'll just wait for the next flight out."

Caroline knew he was being cautious. She took his lead and said, "I suppose since they are responsible for us missing the flight that they are also responsible for our overnight stay if there is no other flight out today."

"Of course. We may enjoy another day here," he said trying to hide his anxiety.

They both picked up a magazine but their thoughts were not on the magazine's contents. Caroline felt sure that they would be caught. She tried her best not to panic. She kept looking at Jean for comfort but he avoided her eyes. He didn't speak Hebrew and knew that they were in serious trouble. If they double-checked the passports with the Israeli passport office they would know that they were fake. His thoughts turned to escape. Could they get out of the office and the airport without being stopped? Just then the immigrations officer returned.

"I'm afraid our meeting will be delayed. The gentleman that was going to speak with you is not coming in today. He will be here first thing in the morning. I'll make arrangements for your overnight stay. Unfortunately your bags were already onboard and you will have to do without them for the night, so we will give you a voucher for the necessities you require for the night. Just relax while we make the arrangements. I'll hold onto your passports and return them when you return tomorrow. Mr. Jones will escort you to a courtesy airport shuttle to the hotel."

"Thank you, sir," said Jean. We appreciate it."

"Will it be separate rooms or do you prefer sharing the same room? He said raising his eyebrows.

"The same room," said Jean with a smirk.

The relief showed on both their faces. Jean looked at Caroline smiling and she returned it.

It didn't take long and they were escorted to the exit where a shuttle bus from the Marriott hotel was waiting.

"You are expected to return to our office at 9 a.m. tomorrow," said the security assistant.

They got on board the bus and said nothing during the short trip to the hotel. Their rooms were ready. All they had to do was sign the register and they were handed a key. They avoided the elevator and took the stairs to the third floor. Jean didn't want to be in the confines of an elevator and have to acknowledge the presence of other hotel guests. Escape was his focus and quick action was required.

***

Richard was in the office early waiting for Samantha's call. He and Mary had talked most of the night and had finally fallen asleep shortly before his alarm clock sounded. He still didn't know what he should do. He kept remembering Mary saying how she wished it was they who had left, or that they could have gone with James and Brenda. Mary did not want to carry out the mission. That was quite clear. What should he tell Samantha? He was placed in charge and they were depending on him. How could he refuse to carry out the mission?

Joyce had completed her work on time as promised. She was pleased with herself and he congratulated her on a job well done. He decided to give her a cash bonus and handed it to her as she was leaving the office. She would not be coming into the office today and that would allow him complete privacy. The shipment to Henry Lerew with a third of the total prepared substances had been made and he was waiting to hear from Henry that it had arrived. The status of the southern teams had not been discussed with him however he assumed that part of the shipment to Henry would be shared with Team #4, not knowing that Team #4 ceased to exist. He sat alone, nervously awaiting the call from Samantha. He must inform her that Team #2 ceased to exist and was hoping that something would happen to cancel the entire mission. Mary's reluctance mirrored his own.

***

Samantha sat at the telephone ready to make the call to Albert. David asked her to give the order to commence with the infestation. She first wanted confirmation that the shipment had been made to Henry and that the work was finished at Ithaca. Once the order was given, Albert would be ordered to shut down the office, leaving no traces behind. The First and Second teams were to place the viruses at the planned locations and then disappear from the area. There were just three days remaining on their visas. The time was short but that was advantageous. When they went into action their minds would be focused on getting the job done without time for reflection or second thoughts. Staying focused on the desire for retribution was now the problem, and that would soon become evident.

Albert answered the phone as usual, identifying himself as Altman.

"Is this Richard Altman?"

"Who's calling please?"

"It's Arnold Myers. I'm calling for Richard Altman."

"Hello Arnold, this is a surprise. How did you get my number?"

"That's a long story requiring a lot of detective work and a bit of luck. But at last I found you. I would like to see you and thought perhaps I could pop by your office. Are you free? I could be there in a few minutes."

"Actually, Arnold, I'm very busy at the moment. It may be better if I call you and we can arrange a time to meet. I have your phone number. And how is Silvia?"

"Fine, fine Richard. I'll tell her you asked. When can I expect your call?

"I will call you within the next few days so we can get together. Can you wait a few days?"

"Of course. I waited this long, a few more days won't make much difference. But please call. There's a lot to discuss. And please give Mary my regards."

"Will do. Got to run. Goodbye Arnold."

He no sooner hung up the phone with Arnold when it rang again.

"Altman here," said Richard.

"This is Samantha. I tried calling you a few minutes ago but your line was busy. Is everything Okay?"

"No, not really. We've got a few issues."

"Issues? What kind?"

"That phone call was from a man that Mary and I had met some time ago and he has tracked me down. He's been asking lots of questions and could cause some problems. I put him off for a few days, but that's not the big problem."

"What's the big problem?"

"I'm sorry to tell you this, but James and Brenda left last night. They're on their way home."

There was a brief silence, and then Samantha said, "Just a moment."

Albert held while Samantha told David what Albert had said. David covered his eyes with both hands. Now instead of four teams he now had just two. David uncovered his eyes and said, "Ask him if the material was sent to Team #3."

Samantha came back on the line and asked Albert if he had sent the material to Team #3 as requested.

"Yes, it was sent. I'm waiting for confirmation that it was received. It should be there today."

"I'm not going to ask the reasons why Team #2 left since they obviously had a change of heart. What I need to know is how you feel. Are you willing to carry out your assignment or are you having second thoughts also?"

Albert was silent. He wasn't sure what to say or do. She had been so kind to him. They had become friends over the course of months and now at the eleventh hour he may let her down. He knew also that she was working for someone else and it wasn't just letting her down but everyone involved in the mission. He felt that telling only the truth was the right thing to do. He said, "My partner and I have had discussed the matter the entire night after our friends departed, and I must admit that we are not as keen about it as we once were."

Samantha did not hesitate. "Let me call you back. I need to discuss this with my boss. I will also call Team #3 and see if the material arrived. Do nothing until I call you back." The connection went dead.

David had been listening in. As soon as she hung up she said, "Team #4 must have departed since their phone is no longer in service. Of course we expected that. Team #2 has now departed and Team #1 is wavering. What do you suggest, David?"

"Contact Team #3 and see if they are waffling also. I don't think we can count on anything now. The mission may have to be scrubbed."

It was almost as though Henry had been sitting by the phone waiting for a call. He answered the phone after the first ring. When Samantha had identified herself, his first words were, "We're ready."

"Did you receive the package," asked Samantha.

"Yes, it came this morning. I opened it and it appears to be more than we need here. Did you want me to send some further south?"

"No, that won't be necessary."

"Fine. I can find a place to use it in this area. When do we begin?"

"Are you and your partner ready to proceed without any reservation?"

"Of course. That's what we came here for and we want to get on with it. You must be aware that our time here is running out. We need to act fast."

"I'll call you back within the hour and let you know what happens next," she said.

Samantha hung up the phone and turned to David. "The material arrived and he is ready to begin. There was no indecisiveness on his part. What do you suggest?"

"I don't want to give Albert the order to begin. His heart is not in it and he will regret it for the rest of his life. It will also make him vulnerable should he ever be questioned. I want you to call Albert and tell him to dispose of all documents and material. He should not contact anyone and leave without delay. He should take whatever cash he needs and then close the account." He paused and then said, "Tell him that I appreciate the work he has done and that I want to wish him and Mary all the best for the future."

Samantha made the call. Albert was pleased at the instructions he received. It was such a relief to him that his emotions surfaced

With a choking voice he said, "Thank you. I'm sorry things didn't work out as planned, but I appreciate the decision you have made. I know my partner will be relieved to hear it. Just so you know, we have learned much from being here. I think we can use this experience to help our people. I will do everything you have asked and leave. Thanks again." he said and hung up.

Albert wasted no time. He called Mary and asked her to pack a bag for each of them and to be prepared to leave as soon as he got home. He cleaned out all the materials in the Lab. His small lab didn't have all the centrifuges, incubators, fridges, cell culture media, sterile plastic materials and hood that were required under normal conditions. Much of the work had been handled at the private lab by the scientist. Any remaining material that could give evidence of the work they did was removed. He carefully packed the virus materials into cool boxes in a way similar to the way he had used for the shipment to South Carolina. The garbage was not separated but taken to a large depot where it was dumped and then backfilled. He carried the material outside to the large dumpster that serviced the office complex. After that he prepared a letter to the landlord canceling the office lease and telling them to keep the deposit. He left a note on the desk telling the landlord to keep the office furnishings or dispose of it as they wished. He gave no explanation.

He called a taxi. On the way out of the building he deposited the office key in the letter slot of the main entrance. He directed the taxi to his bank where he took out what he felt was enough money to get them home. Half of it he would give to Mary to carry and avoid any problem with security. He asked the taxi to wait when he reached his apartment. He hurried up the walk and saw that Mary was ready and waiting. He kissed her and said, "We're leaving."

Mary picked up her bag to follow, then stopped. She turned around and looked once more at the house they had occupied as their home. Albert waited for her to face him again. When she did, her eyes were misty. She said nothing and followed him to the waiting taxi.

***

The call Henry received from Samantha made him furious. Having worked to survey the area, make the identification of the locations for infestation, waiting for the material to come, and then, once it arrived, to cancel? That made no sense. "Why have we trained, if not to carry out the mission?" he asked Simone.

Simone was perplexed seeing how much it affected Henry and although she felt a bit of relief at the decision, she would never admit that to him. They were partners, a team, and she had hopes for a future together. She would do whatever Henry decided.

Samantha had ordered Henry to take the materials he had received and bury them. It was the safe thing to do; however, he had no intention of burying them. In his mind the mission was not yet over.

After Samantha got off the phone with Henry, she felt relief. It was almost as though she had been carrying a heavy load on her shoulders and now it was gone. Her personal feelings of retaliation had diminished when she and David acknowledged their love for one another. Now it was over and she was with David. She walked over and embraced him. "It's over David," she said.

"Yes, it's over. Now it's just you and me." He kissed her and then said, "We will go somewhere we cannot be found."

"And where's that?"

"I always had a place in mind but was never sure until you arrived carrying that Bavarian hat. It was your gift that made my decision. We'll go to the Bavarian Alps."

Samantha laughed out loud. It felt so good and yet funny picturing David standing in the Alps wearing that hat. "I like that," she said. "When do we leave?"

"As soon as I have cancelled all phone and bank connections used for the teams. What about your phones?"

"After getting a disconnect from Jean and Caroline, I cancelled the phone number they were given to contact me. Phone connections to other teams I'll do now."

"Good. After we make these calls we'll leave, but it won't be easy. The Mossad are looking for me and it will require some special tactics to get past security - especially Interpol. We cannot rush it."

***

As soon as they got in their room at the Marriott, Jean said, "We must leave at once. If we showed up tomorrow we'd be arrested."

"But," said Caroline, "They have our passports. We won't be able to leave the country without them."

"They'll discover that we have false papers and be waiting for us. Our passports won't do us any good now. We got to get away from here while we have the chance. Go downstairs and purchase whatever you think we'll need for the next few days. Buy a hat for yourself that will cover most of your face, or at least something where you can tuck in your hair. Get some makeup – something that will help to change your appearance. Buy a baseball cap for me. I'll find something else later. Ask for a small bag to carry what you purchase and charge everything to the room."

"Oh Jean," Caroline said with tears in her eyes, "all our plans. What will we do? How will we live?"

"We'll manage somehow. I'll try to contact Samantha. Perhaps she can help us. I can't call her from this room since they will trace the call. While you're getting the things I'll go downstairs and find a public phone. Do it now. We can't afford to wait. Every minute counts."

Jean didn't want to worry Caroline unnecessarily but he knew his chances of reaching Samantha were a long shot. She had always called him and the number she had given him for emergencies he had never used. This was certainly an emergency. Even so, if she didn't answer the phone, he couldn't leave a number for her to reach him. He had already given up the key to their apartment and cancelled the phone service.

He located the public phones but they required a credit card to use. He was advised never to use the card to phone Samantha since it was too easy to trace. But he had no choice. He inserted the card and dialed. He let the phone ring at least 15 times but there was no answer. Jean checked the phone book for the address of the nearest branch of the Wachovia bank and then returned to the room. Where to go in an emergency had not been a concern. Samantha would provide instructions for such an event. He had no car and would have to rely on public transportation. Renting a car now would only provide an immediate trace for the police. He needed cash. The bank would be his first stop.

Caroline returned carrying two small canvas shopping bags. Jean didn't asked what she bought, just said, "Use the toilet, apply your makeup and then we'll leave."

Caroline came out of the bathroom with her hair tucked into a wide-brimmed hat. She had applied heavy makeup, something she never did, and it made her look rather strange. It brought a smile to his face and she returned it with a small giggle. She handed him an Atlanta Braves baseball cap. He adjusted the size strap and put it on as he headed for the door.

They took the stairway, and once outside he pulled the bill of his cap down to cover most of his face and went to the taxi stand. He gave the address of the Wachovia bank to the driver and they were off. His thoughts were racing. He must take out enough funds to sustain them for an unknown period of time. He wasn't sure if there would be a second chance to withdraw money once the pursuit began. He didn't know if there was a limitation placed on the amount of any withdrawal, but he would chance it. The banks were already closed for the day so the ATM was the only choice. He had just this one chance to access it without suspicion; afterward it could be risky. There had never been a problem procuring what he needed for his living and travel expenses, but that was without any pressure and the amounts he withdrew were modest. It is possible, he thought, that arrangements were made to exceed normal limit of $500.

When they reached the bank he told the driver he would be just a few minutes. He walked to the ATM and inserted his card. He pressed the withdrawal key and then stopped before typing in the amount. It occurred to him that he might be better off pulling out a smaller amount and then proceed to the next Wachovia bank with a different taxi. He punched in $1000. The machine hummed and clicked, and then the money started pumping out in $20's. He stuffed the stack of fifty bills in his pocket, returned to the taxi, and instructed the driver to take them to the train station.

The Amtrak train for the day had already departed. There wouldn't be another until 8:21 p.m. the next day. He took another taxi to the Greyhound bus terminal. There was a bus leaving at 1:30 a.m. bound for Baltimore, Maryland. The ticket window was open and he booked two seats. It was 11:30 p.m. and he realized that they had not eaten any dinner since they had expected to eat on the plane. He took Caroline by the arm and they walked several blocks before locating an all-night fast food restaurant. As soon as they were seated, Caroline said, "Do you think we could travel to Simone and Henry? Perhaps they could help us."

"That's a good idea, but I want to try reaching Samantha again. If we show up at Simone and Henry's place it could place them in jeopardy. We've got to try and sort things out ourselves. That's what all the training was about. Before the bus leaves, I'll try using the ATM at the terminal to see if I can get more money."

"I still have money from your last withdrawal. I didn't use all you gave me for food. I have around $200. How much did you have with you, not counting what you just withdrew?"

"About $500. I thought we wouldn't need more dollars since we were leaving the country. I planned to get what we needed when we arrived in Paris."

"That means that we have about $1700 in total."

"Not exactly. It cost $200 for our bus fare. So we've got more like $1500. I must get more money before our account is closed. I'll try again before we leave and then again when we get to Baltimore. If I can reach Samantha, she may have a solution for us."

CHAPTER 19
THE LAST DAYS

Albert and Mary took the first flight out of Ithaca. It was on US Airways and headed to Philadelphia. Once they were airborne there was a sense of relief for Albert. He couldn't help but reflect on events of the past several days. He was glad that he had paid Joyce and gave her the bonus. He knew she would not understand his sudden disappearance and the close of the office. He thought about Arnold and what he would do when there was no contact as promised. He tried to think of anything he had failed to do that would leave a trace. He was pleased not to know of any.

In Philadelphia they were able to catch a flight to Toronto. Since they were leaving the country, their passports were reviewed to make sure they were valid. Traveling to Canada instead of Europe allowed them to proceed on board without any special scrutiny, and there was no problem passing through Canadian customs control in Toronto. Albert and Mary's tickets were with Air Canada, and all flights to Europe for the next day were fully booked. They were placed on stand-by although they told there was not much chance for any seats soon. For the following day there was only one seat available and Alfred reserved that for Mary. She argued that she would not leave without him but then conceded. He felt that with one confirmed seat, and since they were traveling together, there was a better chance for him to get onboard. He also made the argument with the reservations agent that his visa would expire unless he got on the flight. She told him as politely as she could that the problem with his visa was not hers or that of the airline, and that he should have booked his flight earlier or applied for an extension. He acknowledged that it was his fault but said he would appreciate any help she could give.

Using the airport locater, Albert found a nearby hotel with airport service. After checking in, they went to dinner where they discussed the situation concerning the flight. Mary was finally convinced to take her reserved seat and leave without him if nothing became available. He would apply for an extension first thing in the morning with the Canadian immigration service. He didn't know if traveling alone would make him more conspicuous but there may not be a choice. There was some solace knowing that they had not carried out any terrorist acts and were therefore not guilty of anything other than traveling with false identity papers. There was also the comfort factor of traveling with Mary, and the thought of her going alone made him nervous. Yes, he was in love with Mary. They had lived together as husband and wife. He wanted to make that legal when possible. Where they would live and what identity they would have was still unclear. For the time being, they would stay in Germany, but they had to get there first.

***

Henry knew his time was running out. He had to act quickly or request an extension for his visa. If he got one, he would have time to do a thorough job in his targeted locale with enough virus material left over to spread it to others. Yes, that's what he would do. He didn't come all this way to stop now. Just because the other teams chickened out didn't mean that he would. No, he would show them what he was made of. Someone had to teach these Americans a lesson and he would do it, but he needed more time to do the job right. He must get an extension before his visa expired in two days. Tomorrow he would go with Simone to the immigration service at the airport and request an extra one or two weeks. "I don't see any reason why they would not grant us an extension if we have a good reason," he said to Simone.

"What reason will you give?"

"That you have become sick and are unable to travel," he said.

"And what sickness will I have that will keep me from traveling?"

"I don't know. Perhaps you could think of some female thing that could prevent you from traveling."

Simone broke out laughing, and then said, "But what about you? Just because I can't travel doesn't mean that you can't. Since we're not married they may think it isn't necessary for you to stay."

"You're right, I didn't think of that. I also considered breaking an arm or leg, but we both can't have broken arms or legs, how would we complete the mission? No, that won't do. I suppose I could at least inquire. That way we will know for sure."

"Isn't it possible to call? Must we go there?"

"Good idea," he said and picked up the phone directory. He found the number and placed the call. He got a recording stating the office hours, and then there were questions about the nature of the call. He was to press a particular number if the options they gave applied to his question. None of them did. After trying the same number again and waiting until the end of the options, he was told to stay on the line and an operator would answer. He waited and then there was another recording saying that all the lines were busy, but to stay on the line or call back at another time. Not wanting to go through the same procedure again, he decided to stay on the line. Every so often the same message would be repeated and Henry was becoming frustrated to the point of being angry. Finally an operator answered with, "May I help you?"

"Yes. I need to speak to an immigrations officer because my visa is expiring."

"I'm sorry sir, but there is no one in that office now. They have gone for the day. You'll have to call back tomorrow. The office hours are from 9 to 12 a.m. and from 2 to 4 p.m."

Henry hung up the phone before getting the address of the office. The address he could find through information but time was working against him. Even if he had reached someone they would still have to present themselves at the office to get the documents stamped, assuming that they would be approved. He had no choice but to wait until tomorrow. He decided to take Simone and go out for dinner. It would help to occupy the time and get their minds onto something else.

Since they had no reservations, they were seated in the bar section of the restaurant to wait until a table became available, and they ordered a drink. On the TV monitor the news was in progress. Suddenly there was a special news bulletin from Homeland Security:

> *"We have reason to believe that a terrorist attack against America may be imminent. We don't know where the attack will take place but all security services are on full alert. Airport security has been tightened and passports being scrutinized for possible forgeries. It is believed that both men and women may be involved. They are suspected to be of Middle Eastern origin and may be using aliases. Any unusual activity by persons unknown to you should be reported at once at the number shown below."*

They both sat riveted to the TV. Simone had grabbed his hand and her fingernails were digging into his skin. He wanted to get up and run out of there but now more than ever they needed to remain calm. Instead of drawing attention by leaving, they waited until their seat was available and followed the waitress to their table. As soon as they were seated, Henry said, "This changes everything. Trying to get an extension now would be walking directly into trouble. Let's eat and go home."

They had no appetite and just picked at their food. After a reasonable period of time, he asked for the check and they went back to their room.

***

Arnold and Silvia Myers had gone out to their favorite restaurant. It was customary for them to first have a drink in the bar before being seated. The news bulletin from Homeland Security caused him to sit on the edge of his seat. Could it be? he thought. Could Richard be part of this? He downed his drink in one gulp. He decided not to say anything to Silvia. He would go to Richard's office in the morning and see if he was still there. Richard had not called him as he had promised. If Richard is not there, he thought, I will call Homeland Security. There are just too many questions about his business - especially with all the secrecy. I wonder what he's up to. I've got to find out.

***

David carried several passports with separate identities. Samantha carried two. She had a Lebanese one and a German one. She had refused to carry an Israeli passport for personal reasons. Her German Passport and ID were provided to her when she was in Germany for the team training and she had used that for traveling to the USA. Now that they were planning to go to the

211

Bavarian Alps, having German identity was beneficial. Getting there was another matter. David knew that a direct flight to one's final destination would be foolish if they were to disappear without a trace. He therefore had devised a roundabout route and they were now traveling north, having decided to visit Niagara Falls before entering Canada.

They had a wonderful day. Samantha was thrilled with the Falls and the romantic atmosphere. They decided to stay overnight and then proceed into Canada the following morning. When Samantha went to take a bath, David turned on the TV. He was just in time to hear the news bulletin from Homeland Security. His last message from Natasha caused him to believe that security would be put on the alert looking for him. He suspected that they also might have put out an alert looking for persons entering the USA of Middle Eastern origin. The news bulletin referencing forged passports was another indication that they knew more about his involvement and now suspected that his team had traveled to the USA. This public announcement would have made it difficult for the team members to move about if they had remained. He only hoped that they had all gotten out before this announcement. He was concerned that some of his team may have been detained trying to leave.

He was powerless to do anything about that now. His concern was for Samantha and himself. They would not enter Canada and take that risk. For the moment, it would be safer to sit tight until the scare died down since no act of terror would be carried out. He would not tell Samantha about the news bulletin and ruin the evening. He would wait until tomorrow and then they could head southwest toward California and the Mexican border.

***

Albert accompanied Mary to the airport for her departure to Frankfurt. Although he was still on standby, they gave him no hope for a seat. He would be listed as priority for a seat on the following day – one day after his visa expired. He would wait until Mary's flight departed and then go to immigration to get the extension. They had seen Mary's passport when she checked-in and she had been given her boarding pass. Now they stood together outside the security area as long as possible. She would need to hurry if she were to get through security and be at the departure lounge in time. It was decided that Mary would take a room near the Frankfurt airport and wait for him to arrive the following day. She brushed a tear away as they said goodbye and she entered the security area.

Albert walked to the immigration department. He showed his documents to the desk officer and explained his problem. He asked if they would please grant him an extension.

"Mr. Roth. Why did you wait so long to seek a reservation? Certainly you had sufficient time," said the lady officer.

"You're right of course, and I have no excuse. I just assumed that there would be no problem getting a seat. I heard that most flights to Europe always had seats available since there weren't as many tourists flying there. They say it had something to do with the cost of the Euro against the dollar."

"That may be true, Mr. Roth, but that doesn't relieve you of the responsibility to make reservations."

"No, it doesn't, and I apologize."

She studied his passport looking at him and then again at it. She picked a pamphlet and began reading it, again looking at his passport. "Please have a seat, Mr. Roth. I'll be back in a few minutes."

She left the room carrying his passport and went into a back office closing the door. Albert became worried. Did they suspect that his papers were forged? Had someone notified them about the mission? He turned inward, remembering his training. He must remain calm and not show his nervousness. That would cause them to be more suspicious. Relax, he told himself. It is their job to be suspicious. If they know something for sure they will act. Otherwise they will simply ask questions.

He picked up a pamphlet and tried to read. It hit him that they might have a hidden camera. By the time the officer returned, he had formed some answers to anticipated questions.

"Mr. Roth. Where were you born?"

"In Augsburg, Germany."

"Where did you spend your time on this visit?"

"I was here with my girlfriend. We wanted to make this trip to learn more about each other and see if we would want to make our relationship permanent. She was able to get a seat and left this morning and will be waiting for me in Frankfurt. The first place we visited was Niagara Falls. I think that did it," he said smiling. It seems that most people visiting the Falls were on their honeymoon. Of course we visited the sites here in Toronto including the CN Tower first. It was a clear day and we could see all the way to the Falls before we traveled there."

"That would only account for a few days. Where else did you go?"

"After visiting the Falls we decided to take a tour south and visit New York City. We spent most of the time in America, I'm ashamed to say."

The officer noticed the stamp in his passport denoting when he had entered the USA and then the further stamp entering Canada. Everything seemed to be in order, so she said, "Mr. Roth. Where can you be reached?"

"At the Holiday, Room 3A."

"I will issue you a three-day extension. That should allow you sufficient time to catch a flight. If I have any further questions, I'll contact you there. And I wish you all the best with your marriage."

"Thank you, ma'am, for the extension and for your best wishes. I appreciate it," he said and left the building. The relief he felt was difficult to contain. He waited until he was out of sight and then stopped, wiped his brow and took a few minutes to settle his nerves. Then he went to Air Canada to make his reservation.

***

Jean waited until after midnight before using the ATM. He tried again for $1000. It was rejected. He tried for $500. That too was rejected. He tried the third time for $200. Also declined. He said nothing to Caroline about his failure and boarded the waiting bus. He was exhausted. Shortly after the bus got underway he fell asleep with Caroline leaning on his shoulder.

The Immigrations Officer didn't wait until the next day. He had but placed a check on the passports. He submitted a request to the Israeli Passport Office for confirmation of passport numbers and corresponding names. The answer came back within a few hours stating that no passports with those names had been issued and that the numbers used on the passports were assigned to someone else. The passports were fraudulent.

The Immigrations Officer wasted no time. He sent a security team to the hotel to pick them up for further questioning. The call he received from security confirmed his suspicions. Jean Dupont and Caroline Bardot had skipped out. He immediately sent a report to Homeland Security about the discrepancy with persons carrying Israeli passports and their disappearance. The police were notified and the search began.

CHAPTER 20
TERRORIST ALERT

Henry reviewed the handling instructions in front of him. He decided on a method to infect his designated area based on the original plan. Simone would be his lookout while he placed the virus as instructed. From his calculations, he would have material left over that he could use elsewhere and he was determined to use all of it. He knew that it was highly contagious and it only required a small amount to spread.

"We will begin tomorrow," he said to Simone. "There's no reason to wait and I want to get it done. After that we can leave the area. We will be far away when things begin to happen here, but we will have avenged our families. We will have made these people pay. Their government is responsible for the destruction of our country and the lives of our people. Simone, I think you should know that we will need to find work to survive. I don't have much money left and the lease on the apartment will expire in a few days. By that time we must be away from here."

Simone did not reply. She was already thinking about how they would survive without the proper papers to get work, but she was placing her future in Henry's hands. She loved him and was confident he would find a way. She didn't want to think about the results of the actions they were about to take. She knew that many people would die.

***

David and Samantha were on their way to the Southwest. Everything was new and exciting to Samantha. Being in love and traveling with David without cause for any immediate worry gave her a feeling of euphoria. All the hate she had harbored for so many years had slipped away. She was at peace with herself and life felt good. Her need for vengeance was gone. The people they had occasion to meet as they traveled west were pleasant and had a ready smile. She could go on like this forever, she thought. Occasionally she would think about the team members and how fond she had become of them. To see them fall in love with their partners was something pleasant to remember. She wondered if they had all been able to leave the country safely. Would she ever see them again? Would she ever learn their fate? That was doubtful. She and David would live in a remote village somewhere in the Alps, but first they had to get there.

In three days they had reached Los Angeles. They found a nice quiet motel near the beach and enjoyed a day of leisure, swimming and laying in the sun. They took a tour of Hollywood and got to see some of the mansions of famous movie stars. David picked up a newspaper and stopped abruptly as he read the front page:

Suspected Terrorist Plot

Since the news broadcast from Homeland Security's special news bulletin about a suspected terrorist plot, (bulletin shown below) they have received numerous calls from people about suspicious persons and their actions. Homeland Security says they will follow up on all these leads even though most or all may lead nowhere. 'It is just too great a risk not to take any lead seriously,' said a spokesman.

David stopped reading and handed the paper to Samantha. Nothing was said as they returned to their motel and packed their belongings.

They traveled south along the coast to the Mexicali border crossing. What normally would have been a pleasant trip enjoying the new surroundings was changed to one of haste in crossing the border into Mexico. There were just two cars in front of them when they reached the border. The officer didn't spend much time with either car and then motioned for David to approach. He presented his American passport and Samantha's German passport. The customs officer looked at the passports and then at their faces to ascertain they were the same.

"What's the purpose of your trip to Mexico," he asked.

"We're on a holiday, sir."

"How long do you plan to stay?"

"It depends on the weather. We expect two weeks."

The officer handed back the passports with a nod and said, "Enjoy your stay."

David drove to the nearby Mexicali airport intending to turn in his rental car and rent another one for the trip to Mexico City. He had changed cars in Los Angeles since he didn't want the car in Mexico traced back to Philadelphia. The rental cars available at this small airport were not late models and those available were without air conditioning. Driving through Mexico without AC was not something he wanted to do. So he booked a flight to Mexico City. He discarded everything he no longer needed in the nearest garbage bin, including the serum vials of virus antidotes. It was a small plane that had seen many years of use and would make several stops en route, but it would get them there. They were looking forward to a bit of relaxation in Mexico City before making further travel arrangements. Nothing was planned in advance.

Being flexible and taking advantage of opportunities was the best strategy from this point forward. They were now out of the USA but caution was not discarded.

When they landed in Mexico City, David checked for accommodations. The list of hotels were varied and most offered a shuttle service. He decided on the Best Western Hotel. It would provide good comfort with AC and make them less visible than that of a larger hotel. He purchased an English language newspaper and then hailed a cab. He scanned the paper searching for any reports concerning the suspected terror threat, but there was nothing. That was to their advantage. 'Out of sight, out of mind' was analogous to 'out of the news, out of one's mind,' and they could move more freely.

***

In Ithaca, Arnold knocked on the office door for Richard but there was no answer. He inquired at the office next door and asked if they had seen anyone entering or leaving office #8.

"No, sir. I think that office is now empty. You might want to check with the landlord."

"Empty? When did they move out?"

"I'm not sure. We haven't seen anyone for the past two or three days."

Arnold checked with the landlord and was told that the office was now vacant.

"Do you know where they went?" said Arnold.

"No. We received a note from Richard Altman saying that he was closing the office, but he left no forwarding address."

"What did they do there?"

"We don't know. When we rented the office to him he said that they would be doing some research work connected with the university. That's all I can tell you. They gave us no problem and it was very quiet there."

The next thing Arnold did was to call Carol. He knew that her roommate Joyce had worked there. Surely she will know something, he thought, but when he called there was no answer. He waited for several hours before calling back, realizing they were most likely attending lectures at the university. When he did call, the phone was answered, "This is Joyce."

"Hello Joyce. This is Arnold Myers. I believe we met at your office. Do you remember?"

"Yes, Mr. Myers."

"I went by the office where you worked but there's no one there. I'm told that the office is closed. Any idea where they went?"

"No, Mr. Myers. I have no idea. They just left without saying anything."

"Did they pay you?"

"Yes, I got paid but without any notice that my work had ended. It really is a puzzle."

"What kind of work did you do?"

"I'm sorry, Mr. Myers, but I was sworn to secrecy. There may be a good reason why they moved out and may still wish to contact me. I will continue to honor my word."

"Well, I find it very strange. Something funny was going on there and I'm not through with this yet. I'm going to the authorities. I don't know if you saw the news broadcast but there might be some connection. You will probably hear from them." He hung up before Joyce could reply.

Joyce was bewildered. She didn't remember hearing anything special on the news. What did he mean by some connection?

Some connection to what? She would ask Carol if she heard anything.

***

The bus slowed to make a sharp turn into the Baltimore depot, awakening Jean. He was alert at once and shook Caroline. "We're here," he said.

Caroline rubbed her eyes and took in the surroundings as the bus came to a stop. A number of people were waiting to greet the arrivals. Off to the side stood two plain clothed policemen observing the people as they stepped down from the bus. There was nothing about their demeanor that looked out of the ordinary and those departing the bus had eyes only for friends waiting to greet them. Jean's concentration was on his immediate need to call Samantha and searched for directional signs to telephone and toilet facilities. As they stepped down from the bus the two men waiting closed in on them.

"Come this way please," said the officer while flashing his police badge.

Jean knew it was useless to resist. He took Caroline by the arm as they were ushered from the depot to a waiting police car.

"May I please use the toilet," said Caroline.

"I must use it as well," said Jean.

"You can use the facilities at the station," said the officer while opening the door to the car, nudging them inside.

The ride to the station lasted about 15 minutes. Caroline held onto Jean's arm as they rode in silence. She knew it was all over for them. The dream of getting married, of returning to America to live – dreams never to be fulfilled. Jean's mind was active but getting him nowhere. No passports. No other ID. Skipping out had sealed their fate. Now would come the interrogation. There was no plausible explanation. Silence was the only defense to protect the other team members. He would do his best to uphold his pledge.

***

Henry and Simone placed the virus material in the trunk of their car and were on their way. It wasn't far to travel before they turned off the highway onto a dirt road that led into the forest. They continued along the pre-planned route to where they would park. From there they would go on foot. They passed no cars on the way in and the spot where they planned to park was empty. "So far, so good," said Henry. "This may work out just as planned."

Henry put on his backpack. It was already filled with the virus container. He stuck his handgun in the pocket of his vest. He handed Simone the second backpack to carry that he would use when the first one was empty. Simone's job was to walk ahead to scout the area to be infested and then give a signal that it was clear before Henry would place the packets of virus foodstuffs in the feeding areas. She checked on the first site and then with her birdcall, let Henry know that it was safe to proceed. She stood a distance away while he performed the work to make sure no one was watching. When he was finished, he gave a signal on his birdcall and she moved to the next area. The paths to these areas were marked as they had learned to do when they were training in the Vosges mountain range in France. As Simone stood watch, she reflected on those training days that seemed a long time ago. So much had happened since that time.

She remembered the first time she and Henry had met. Samantha had arranged for dinner where they could meet each other. She had been timid and shy but Henry had made her feel important. She liked him from the very beginning. He was handsome with a zest for life and for the mission. He was ready to tackle the Americans single-handed if necessary. Much of his passion rubbed off on her. Before they began living together she had imagined what it would be like for the two of them to share that passion in bed, and she didn't have long to wait. Remembering that night always brought back memories that made her blush. She liked the way he spoke to her of love in French. Yes, they were meant for each other. They were a team and she would stick by him.

Her thoughts were interrupted when she heard his signal. The next area was by a branch of the Reedy River where he deposited the fish virus. She advanced toward the next to last spot on their list. Her mind was still on past events and she had not noticed the person standing directly ahead of her until she was almost on him. She stood perfectly still waiting for the person to move on. The person didn't move but kept looking at her. He then advanced toward her with a mischievous grin on his face. In his right hand he held a gun. She couldn't tell if it was a shotgun or a rifle, but that didn't matter. He was armed and she wasn't. She remained standing, hoping he would just keep walking by her. As he approached she noted his beard and assumed he was much older until he was directly in front of her. He was younger than he had appeared and his smile turned into a mischievous grin.

"What have we here?" He said. "Are you lost, Miss?"

"No, I'm not lost. Just taking a walk through the woods."

"Walking alone in the woods, eh? Perhaps you were looking for me," he said still grinning. "What's that you're carrying in your backpack? You wouldn't have the makings of a picnic now, would you? Let's take a look."

Simone pulled back. There was no way she would let him look inside. He may accidentally open a packet and they could both become infected. She reached for her whistle and blew. It wasn't the signal that Henry would be expecting, but rather one of panic – an indication of trouble.

"What you doing there, Miss? What kind of whistle is that? Give it to me."

Simone again pulled back and the man grabbed her by the arm. She turned quickly and slipped from his grip.

"Now, Miss. We can do this the easy way or the hard way. I won't hurt you. I'll be gentle. You know you want it. Besides, you're trespassing on my property and on my property I have all the rights. And after we're done, I'll take you to my private still and we'll have a drink. What do you say?"

Henry heard the whistle and was making his way toward Simone. He was being cautious, making as little noise as possible, trying to ascertain what the problem might be. And then he heard Simone's voice.

She shouted, "Leave me alone," and bolted. Not fast enough. He grabbed her - started pulling her to him. She kneed him hard in the groin. He bent over groaning. Up came his gun.

"You bitch! You'll pay for this. Stay right where you are or I'll fill that pretty ass of yours with lead."

Simone stopped. She was ready to defend herself if he came near. She didn't see Henry coming but heard him yell, "Drop that gun!"

The man swung around and saw Henry standing with his gun leveled at him. Instead of dropping his gun the man raised it to fire. Henry was quicker. One shot and the man went down. Henry checked to make sure he was dead.

"Come. Let's get out of here."

With adrenaline pumping, they raced to their car. They tossed their backpacks in the trunk and cautiously drove back to the main road. Only after reaching the highway did they speak, and it was Simone who spoke first.

"Was it necessary, Henry?"

"Yes. I had no choice. He was preparing to fire."

"What do we do now?"

"We continue what we started. By the time they find the body we'll be gone.

Just ten miles away was the large chicken farm that Henry had designated as part of the plan, but it had not been included for today's work. Now that their scheme had been foiled, he decided to drive by to see if there was any possibility of doing it now. The stench from the chicken barns reached them even before he had stopped the car. The chickens were housed in four large barns with thousands of chickens in each. Feeding was handled automatically on conveyor belts. He needed to get to the feed supply source and dump some of the virus into the feed. A long driveway led to the barns. There was a separate shed with a tractor and wagon standing alongside, most likely used to transport feed. There was also a small house trailer, presumably for hired help. He saw no one outside. Either they were on break or were working inside the barns. He decided to drive to the shed and park the car there. He would check to see where the personnel were and create some diversion so that Simone could enter the feeding shed. This approach in broad daylight was different from his original plan of stealth at nighttime. The setback caused by the news bulletin induced him to be more aggressive and less cautious. He explained his impromptu strategy to Simone as he started down the driveway.

There was still no one in sight when he pulled alongside the feed shed. He told Simone to stay sitting until he gave her a signal that it was clear. He peeked into the feed shed. It was empty. He walked to the trailer and knocked on the door. No answer. He went to the first of four barns and looked inside. Lots of chicken noise and stench, but no one in sight. When he came outside he motioned for Simone to go into the feed shed. He continued to the second shed and still no one to be seen. At the third barn he stopped before entering and noticed that Simone was no longer in the car. Whatever happened next he needed to keep anyone inside from coming out. That barn was also empty. He was exhilarated as he made his way to the fourth and last barn. What a stroke of luck it would be if that were also empty. He walked inside and saw two men busy working at the far end. Rather than walk to them, he decided to stay where he was until they noticed him. Simone would have enough time to complete the job if they remained in the building a little while longer.

The noise of the chickens drowned out other sounds and he didn't hear the pickup truck coming down the lane. Simone heard it and had dumped the contents of three of the five packets of virus into the feed. She closed her backpack in a hurry without taking the necessary precaution to place the empty packets in a sealed bag. She moved to the door and looked outside as the truck came to a stop next to their car. Where is Henry, she wondered. She stood there as the men went to the back of the truck and opened the tailgate. They were getting ready to pull some bags off the truck when they spotted Henry coming out of the barn. When Henry saw them he stopped and waved and they returned it. He needed to get them away from the feed shed so he stayed where he was and motioned for them to come to the barn. The men stopped what they were doing and started walking toward him. As soon as their backs

ABE F. MARCH

were turned and far enough away, Simone slipped out of the shed and went behind the car holding the backpack close to her chest. The chicken noise drowned out the slight noise of the car door as she got inside and placed the backpack on the backseat. Then she waved to Henry.

"Hello," said Henry.

"Howdy," replied the one and the other acknowledged with a hand wave.

"I didn't see anyone around so I went inside, but the men were so busy I didn't want to bother them."

"What do you want," asked the older of the two.

"Nothing really. My wife and I were driving by and had never been to a chicken farm before. We thought we'd stop and have a look. But I think the smell got to my wife and she went back to the car."

The man turned around and looked at the car and saw Simone sitting there. He looked a bit puzzled, but then said, "Feel free to look around if you like, if you can stand the smell. We're used to it."

"Thanks," said Henry. "I got a peek inside and I think I saw enough. I don't think I can get my wife out of the car again." He laughed and started walking toward the car.

"I don't blame her," said the man. "Have a nice day."

"Thanks, and you also," said Henry, without looking back.

The gun rack in the back window of the pickup truck was not empty but there was no threat. He got into the car without a word and headed back up the driveway. He waited until he reached the main road before he spoke. "Did you do it," he asked.

"I dumped three packets before I heard their truck coming."

"That was enough," he said He reached across and squeezed her arm. "You did well."

***

Arnold Myers didn't remember the phone number for Homeland Security so he went directly to the police station. After he had told them about his suspicions, they got the number for him and helped him place the call. He was transferred to a special agent and answered a series of questions. When he finished, the agent asked to speak to the police chief. Before Arnold left he was asked to give a recorded statement about his suspicions. He was praised for his alertness, for doing his civil duty, and was told that a full investigation would be made. They would be in contact with him for more information as needed. Arnold went home very pleased with himself.

***

Through a network of friends, Natasha got word to her parents that she was safe and that she would arrange for them to join her. She was kept informed about the surveillance of her parent's home, and as long as that continued, she would not risk any move to bring them out. When she learned that the watch had stopped, she still waited a reasonable time to be sure it wasn't some tactic to draw her out before she made her move.

It happened during the busy time of the day. Her mother had gone to market and her father was invited to a friend's house. From the market her mother was taken to a safe house and a short while later her father joined her. They were then escorted separately into the Palestinian territory to another safe house where Natasha was waiting for them. It was a brief but happy reunion. It was not safe living there either, since the Israelis entered the territory at will. The next part of the escape plan was to go to Jordan. Natasha had considered Lebanon but her presence there would present a greater risk of being recognized and because of that she had decided on Jordan. Although Jordan was a monarchy, it was pro-western and people enjoyed freedom as in a democratic state. It was there that Natasha wanted to start a new life. She would live with her parents together with the Arabs.

***

David and Samantha had taken a direct flight from Mexico City to the United Kingdom on British Airways. David was not concerned with the Homeland Security bulletin since he and Samantha were already outside the USA. His main concern was with his own organization, the Mossad. He was acutely aware of their tactics and knew that they would be relentless in their pursuit of him. He had considered an intricate method of getting to Europe but in the end decided to take the unexpected bold move by traveling directly to the UK. There were no difficulties upon arrival at Heathrow airport. He booked a room for an overnight stay in London and then made first class train reservations on Eurostar that would take them to Paris via the English Channel tunnel. There was no reason to hurry and they could enjoy a leisurely trip on the luxurious new train. Samantha was looking forward to visiting Paris as a tourist and her excitement was contagious. David had been to Paris numerous times but he was always alone. Now he would visit this romantic city with the one he loved. He had been careful to use a disguise and make adjustments at each destination. After he left the UK he would no longer need to show a passport while traveling within the European Union (EU) countries that were part of the Schengen agreement, the agreement that abolished border controls. It would thus be easier to change his disguise without it having to agree with his ID, and it gave him a greater sense of freedom. He had his two legitimate passports, one American and one Israeli, under his true name, David Levy. He preferred to carry an Israeli passport while in Europe since it gave him a psychological advantage. The stigma of the Holocaust in Europe was still a strong card to play if stopped for any reason. The simple term, "Anti-Semitic" would give him an edge. The Israeli passport he now carried showed the name, Benjamin Dreyfus. Samantha had her Palestinian passport in her possession but used her German passport that gave her status as an EU resident.

The train trip was pleasant and relaxing. As they dinned, they watched the countryside change from region to region reflecting the cultural differences. The time went by quickly and as they neared Paris, Samantha's excitement grew. The city of love, she thought. What a wonderful place to be with David.

Their arrival at the *Gare de Lyon* train station with all the hustle and bustle was exciting in itself. They easily found a room with a small balcony where they could sit and enjoy the view of the city. It was relaxing to watch the boats make their way down the Seine River. When it turned dark, the glitter of lights illuminated the skyline showing off its famous landmarks, added to the charm. The *Eiffel Tower* looked majestic standing like a pillar amidst the movement of traffic weaving its way through the roundabouts and along the Champs-Elysees Boulevard leading to the *Arc de Triomphe*. They enjoyed Paris oblivious to the infestation that Henry had carried out on his own.

***

Having used all the materials in his possession, Henry had left the infected locales. He was almost out of funds and knew he would face more problems if he continued to drive the leased car that had been placed at his disposal. Someone else had made the payments. With the mission cancelled, he was certain that payments had been stopped, and without payment the lease company would be looking for the car. If it was not returned within a given period of time, and he didn't know how long that was, it would be considered a stolen car. He needed to abandon the vehicle without giving any indication to the direction he was traveling. He wanted to get out of the poisoned territories. He decided to go farther south. They were both accustomed to a warm climate. Without work they may find themselves staying outdoors. These problems had not been considered when he made the decision to stay and carry out the mission on his own. It was now a matter of survival for him and Simone.

They didn't give much thought to the forthcoming disaster they would cause for many others. Simone was not feeling well. She appeared to be getting a cold. At a rest area, they discarded everything except what they could each carry in a backpack. He kept the handgun on his person. The backpack had become contaminated when Simone had thrown the empty virus packets into the bag at the chicken farm. They continued driving until Henry found a secluded spot in a wooded area where he could abandon the car. They took their backpacks and began walking to the nearby town. They were now vagabonds. The few dollars remaining would buy them food for a week if they did not use any of it to pay for lodging.

Simone's flu-like symptoms were getting worse. Henry wasn't felling too well himself. They were not accustomed to going to a doctor for simple illnesses, but Henry was becoming more concerned with Simone. She was getting too tired to walk so he stuck out his thumb to hitch a ride. It was a country road with not much traffic, but a farmer with a pickup truck came toward them driving slowly, and he stopped.

"You folks need a lift?"

"Yes, thank you. We would appreciate a ride to the next town."

"You're welcome to hop on the back. I live just on this side of town. I'll take you that far."

They climbed onto the bed of the truck. It felt good to be sitting rather than walking. Simone was aching all over. Henry tried to be strong and help her, but he too was feeling feverish. He decided to ask the farmer where he might find a doctor in town. After several miles the truck slowed down and came to a stop at a long driveway leading to a farm. Henry got off the truck and helped Simone down. He walked to the door of the cab and thanked the man saying, "We really appreciate the lift. Could you tell me if there is a doctor in town?"

"Is someone sick?"

"Yes, my wife is not well. I think she needs a doctor."

"Well, why don't you just get back on the truck and I'll take you there. You can't have her walking to town if she's sick."

They were relieved that they didn't have to walk the rest of the way. When they got to the doctor's office it was closed.

"Just stay where you are. I'll take you to the hospital. It's just a little way further. They will help you."

When they arrived at the hospital, Henry thanked the farmer and shook his hand. Henry knew hospitals were expensive and that it may take all their money, but that didn't matter. The future was no longer bright. He knew they would have to struggle to survive, but that was nothing new to either of them. They had to struggle all their lives. On top of that, they had lived with the trauma of disaster. They were now in a strange land and on the run as outlaws. What the future held he didn't know, but he needed to take care of the present. Without Simone, he had no future.

***

After arriving at the police station, Jean and Caroline were escorted to the toilet facilities and then placed in separate rooms for interrogation. Waiting was having its affect on both of them. Caroline felt numb. She couldn't believe it would end like this. She kept reminding herself that they had done the right thing. They had not committed any terrorist act. They were simply two people in love that wanted to have a happy life together in America. She tried to ignore the fact that they were guilty by association with the other team members who would carry out the infestation. Jean was having similar thoughts. He was not aware that the mission was cancelled and expected that the actions would be carried out. He felt some relief knowing he was no longer part of the activity but could not deny his association with it. If he said nothing, the attack would occur and millions of people would lose their lives. To squeal on his comrades was not something he wanted to do. And to be silent meant death for many innocent people.

The inquisition began with the interrogators stating what they knew about them. Arriving in America using false passports was a crime. They were informed that they were suspected of being part of a planned terrorist attack on America and wanted information that would prevent such an attack from taking place. "From what we can determine so far, you are guilty of just the one crime. If you cooperate with us, it will work in your favor when it comes time for sentencing. Are you willing to cooperate?"

Jean was prepared for the question and had made his decision. He and Caroline were no longer bent on revenge. They didn't want to see faultless people die. He said, "Yes, I am."

***

David and Samantha left Paris and took a train to Germany. With the convenience of train and bus service they made their way to a small village located on the border of the Bavarian and Austrian Alps. They found accommodations at the Hotel Waldhorn - a sport hotel with indoor recreational facilities. There they could relax, enjoy a swim, have a sauna and take lots of hikes while deciding on a place to live. The view of the Sorgschroffen from their bedroom window was enticing and they decided to climb it. It was a beautiful day, but the trek up the side of the mountain caused them to pause frequently. Benches were placed at intervals for just that purpose and they used them at each stage. David wore his Alpine hat with the red feather and used a climbing stick. Samantha followed him wearing a matching hat that she had purchased at the Ski hut in the valley below. The last stage of the climb was painstakingly slow. David stayed right behind Samantha in case she would lose her footing. It was a matter of using both hands and finding a good foothold before taking the next step in making their way to the top. At the height of almost 2000 meters they had a view of seemingly endless rolling Alps all tipped with snow. They sat on the crest of the mountain watching mountain goats make their way along a cragged path nearby. "I love you," said David.

"I love you, too," said Samantha.

CHAPTER 21
THE ULTIMATUM

Three weeks had gone by. David was looking for a permanent place to live. They both loved the Alps and it was just a matter of finding a suitable place there. On their way to breakfast David picked up the morning paper, as was his habit. He enjoyed the breakfast buffet with the wide variety of food. It was always difficult to decide with so many choices available. Once he had made his selections and sat down, he opened the paper intending to peruse the classified ads. The headline on the front-page caught his attention.

"OUTBREAK OF BIRD FLU IN SOUTH CAROLINA"

David immediately knew the source. The report stated that it had already mutated to a few humans and was causing widespread panic. Without an antidote it was a major disaster in the making.

David put down the paper and sat deep in thought. "Henry and Simone. They didn't dispose of the virus but took it upon themselves to carry out the project. How much of the material did they use," he wondered.

Samantha noticed David had stopped eating, sitting still, holding the paper in front of him. "Is something wrong," she asked.

Without answering, he handed her the newspaper, pointing to the article. When she finished reading it, she said, "The mission was carried out after all."

"Yes, it was. I have no idea how far or how fast it will spread."

He checked other newspapers during the next few days and further news reports stated that the number of people coming down with the flu was increasing on a daily basis and that it had already spread to neighboring states. The first casualties were a young couple from out of town with no identification, who showed up at a local hospital. They had appeared to be suffering from a severe case of the flu. Nothing could be done to stop the continuing spread without an antidote and that was unlikely in a short period of time. It was reported that there appeared to be two sources of the flu virus; one from birds and one from fish. Where evidence of infection was found, farmers were being forced to slaughter all their poultry. The fear of fish contamination had caused people to stop buying fish and fishermen were now concerned about their livelihood.

Homeland security was on high alert. Following up on a tip, they had investigated an office at Ithaca, New York, and had talked with a former employee who had worked with viruses. The employee was persuaded to divulge the type of work she had been doing but she had no knowledge about the disposition of the virus substances. The description of the people associated with the project was sketchy except for a Richard Altman who was reported to be German. It was further suspected that he had ties to the Middle East. A delivery service had confirmed picking up a shipment and sending it to South Carolina. The people to whom it was addressed were no longer living there. Fingerprints were taken and the investigation continued. What was disconcerting was that the outbreak of the virus was in the South.

It was reported that the body of a man had been found in the foothills of the Blue Ridge Mountains outside of Greenville, South Carolina. His death was caused by a single gunshot wound. The virus outbreak was traced to that same place. It was unknown if the dead man was part of the heinous activity or simply someone who got in the way - a victim of murder.

(What they didn't yet know was that the virus that had been placed in the dumpster next to the office in Ithaca would soon infect wildlife in the New York area. There was no mention of the confessions obtained from Jean and Caroline. That information was being held confidential while they continued their investigations).

David finished his breakfast and excused himself while Samantha continued reading the newspaper. He told Samantha that he was going for a walk and needed time to think. He took the path behind the hotel that ran along the hillside that afforded a beautiful view of the valley and the Alps. It was a sunny day and he found a bench to sit on that provided some seclusion. He reflected on past events that had led him to this place. He remembered the major event that had changed his attitude and his loyalty. He had kept this secret to himself, which slowly influenced his thinking and actions. He never thought it would cause him to turn against the country of his birth and the country he had adopted. He had been proud to be a citizen of both countries. When he joined the Mossad organization he thought he would be helping his people with a better life. He remembered what his grandfather had told him about the atrocities against his people and he was determined to help provide a secure place for them to live in peace. Israel was supposed to be that place. He became disillusioned with the work he was asked to do. He questioned many of the actions taken by his organization. The single event that caused him to change was when he was assigned as a security guard at a meeting between an American presidential candidate and a top Israeli political advisor. Hearing an American politician conspiring with an Israeli government representative to defraud the American people and their government out of billions of dollars altered his thinking and affected his loyalty. The American presidential candidate was promised whatever monetary support he needed in his bid for the presidency. What they asked in return was that once he became President he would repay them with aid and loans that the government of Israel would request. In his capacity as President he would see that the loans were "forgiven." The government's representative further indicated that a private offshore bank account would be made available for his personal use, if he so desired.

David knew that it was easy and convenient to provide support to Israel with the backing of the American people since there were ties that bound them together. There were the sympathetic ties caused by the Holocaust. There were the biblical ties by the many religious organizations and then there were the political ties. The support for Israel's existence and their strategic location meant providing them with sophisticated weapons and monetary support. Much of the money was in the form of economic aid and weaponry. What frequently started out as "borrowed money" wound up as "forgiven debts." American politicians knew that the Jewish lobby was strong and money was available if they supported the wishes of Israel. Intimidation was used and most politicians succumbed. The temptation for monetary support to the politicians was often too overwhelming to ignore. They also knew that to talk against Israel was political suicide.

His thoughts were interrupted when a passerby sat down next to him. They exchanged pleasantries and for a few minutes talked about the surroundings and the view. Then the man moved on.

David's thoughts reverted to the reasons he had agreed to undertake the mission. He had hoped that it would serve two purposes: satisfy the desire for revenge by the participants in the mission, and also that they would be the tools to change the existing stalemate between Israel and Palestine. Human suffering on both sides must end. Change could only occur when the citizens would demand that their leaders take the appropriate action.

***

After David had gave the order to destroy the virus there had been no reason to keep the antidote. He had carried it with him as part of his belongings but it became unnecessary baggage. So he had disposed of it in the trash container at the Mexicali airport. Now the antidote was needed to save lives caused by the virus that he was responsible for having created. He and Samantha both knew who had carried out the infestation, and from what they had read, those two had been its first casualties. An antidote was needed to stop untold casualties. David knew the scientists who could re-create it. The antidote could provide a cure if taken within one week of infection. He also knew that taking action to provide the antidote would expose him and his role in the mission. Even before the authorities could press charges against him, he would be vulnerable to liquidation by the Mossad.

It was a no win situation. The justification for the mission was still valid. The basic cause of the problems in the Middle East still existed and was centered on Israel and Palestine. Unless or until that problem was resolved, the bloodshed would continue. "If more people are to die, then they should not die in vain," he said to Samantha.

Samantha didn't respond. What could she say? She observed David as he sat with his elbows propped on his knees, his chin resting on his hands with his eyes closed. She knew he was devising a plan.

David decided to prepare a statement to be published and broadcast on American national television. If the conditions stipulated in the statement were agreed to, he would provide them with the antidote.

STATEMENT

"The major cause of today's terrorism has its roots in Israel. Israel has blatantly refused to abide by UN Resolutions calling for them to cease their occupation of land they seized by war. Israel's continued intransigence in concluding a peace agreement has shown its lack of a desire for peace that is evidenced by the continued building of Israeli settlements in Palestinian territory. The main supporter of Israel is the United States of America both monetarily and politically. America has supplied Israel with weapons that she has used in violation of the conditions of sale. Israel has developed nuclear weapons with stolen plans and materials yet nothing has been done to dispose of her Weapons of Mass Destruction. America's unqualified support for Israel has made her a party to the thousands of lives that have been lost in the region. The entire world has suffered and continues to suffer as a result of Israel's refusal to abide by international law, yet these same laws are enforced on other countries. The world's supply of oil has been continuously affected by this conflict causing economic hardship for millions of people. The oil embargo was a direct result of Israeli intransigence that caused incalculable financial losses around the world. The plight of the Palestinians against injustice has created a bed of resentment toward Israel and America. It is likely that there would not be a reason for today's problem with Iran, Iraq, Syria, and other Arab countries if there were peace between Israel and Palestine. Al Qaeda came into existence as a result of the Israeli-Palestinian problem and the current terrorist activity places its cause at the doorstep of Israel. The illegal *invasion of Iraq was the final act that triggered this current act of terror carried out against America.*

The Virus infestation was a deliberate act to get America's attention but there is an antidote. There is a cure for those infected by the virus and an antidote to stop terrorist acts. To get this antidote, Israel must:

1. Agree to comply with all UN Resolutions

2. Agree to dismantle its nuclear arsenal.

3. Allow UN observers to be stationed between the two territories to insure that both parties honor their commitments.

4. America must agree to enforce the above three points.

This Statement is a warning. The current infestation of birds was a token of what was originally planned. Unless the above legitimate demands are met, others will follow in the footsteps of those who made this infestation. The blame will be solely on those who continue to ignore the legal rights of others.

Be it also known that the availability of the antidote is based on America's decision to act. The responsibility for continued deaths rests with the American government just as the responsibility for the deaths of innocent Palestinians and Iraqis is their responsibility.

It has been stated that America doesn't negotiate with terrorists. This is not a statement for negotiation but an offer for peace."

David carefully typed the "Statement" and placed it in an envelope addressed to The New York Times. He placed that envelope in a larger envelope and addressed that to the International Herald Tribune in Munich. In a cover note to the Herald Tribune marked "urgent," he asked them to open the envelope addressed to The New York Times and to transmit the statement to them. Any reply was to be published in the Herald Tribune.

He took a bus to the train station and boarded the train bound for Munich. In Munich he took a taxi to the office of the Herald Tribune and placed the envelope in their mailbox. With that accomplished, he returned using the same mode of transportation back to the Hotel Waldhorn where Samantha was waiting.

"How did it go, David?" she asked.

"The message is delivered. It is now a matter of waiting for their response. If they agree to do what has been requested, I will do what I promised and get the antidote for them. As you know Samantha, if they do the right thing, it will be the end for us. If they remain obstinate and arrogant, it will be the end for many of them. Their fate and our fate are in their hands."

About the Author

Abraham F. March is an international business consultant and author, living near Landau, Germany with his wife Gisela. An active retiree, he enjoys hiking and exploring the local vineyards and can also be heard singing with a regional men's choir. Mr. March's career has taken him around the world to work in many areas from his birthplace in the USA to Canada, Europe and the Middle East.

His first book, *To Beirut and Back - An American in the Middle East* was published in 2006, and is a memoir of his adventures that took him to Lebanon in the 1970s. Mr. March grew up in York County, Pennsylvania on the family farm, and he served in the USAF from 1957-61. His business career got underway with the computing sciences division of IBM's service bureau where he held positions as manager of administration and operations analyst. He later joined an international cosmetic company where he rapidly achieved top distributor status and was promoted to vice president of sales development and product market management, an opportunity which took throughout the USA and into Canada, Greece, and Germany.

With international experience and an entrepreneurial spirit, Mr. March started his own importing business headquartered in Beirut,

Lebanon, for the distribution of cosmetics and toiletries to the Middle East markets. With an ease about him and a talent for developing business relationships, he also functioned as a locator of goods and services sought by Mid-Eastern clients before the civil war in Lebanon destroyed his successful business enterprise. Mr. March returned to the United States to start over, and was soon working on an international level once again. His subsequent work involved Swan Technologies, Inc., a personal computer manufacturer in West Germany, and back to the US to work with Stork NV, supporting a fleet of 1200 Fokker Aircraft. He officially retired in 2001. *They Plotted Revenge Against America* is his second book.

ALL THINGS THAT MATTER PRESS ™

FOR MORE INFORMATION ON TITLES AVAILABLE FROM
ALL THINGS THAT MATTER PRESS, GO TO
http://allthingsthatmatterpress.com
or contact us at
allthingsthatmatterpress@gmail.com